DATE			

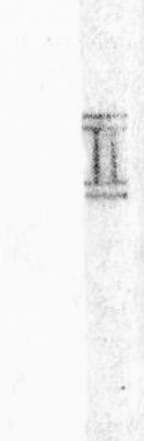

PAPER DAUGHTER

JEANETTE INGOLD

Houghton Mifflin Harcourt
Boston New York 2010

Harcourt is an imprint of Houghton Mifflin Harcourt Publishing Company.

www.hmhbooks.com

Text set in Garamond
Book design by Susanna Vagt

Library of Congress Cataloging-in-Publication Data
Ingold, Jeanette.
Paper daughter / Jeanette Ingold.
p. cm.
Includes historical notes on Chinese immigration to the United States, "paper sons," and the Exclusion Era laws.
Summary: When her father, a respected journalist in Seattle, is killed in a hit-and-run accident, Maggie Chen, a high school intern at her father's newspaper, searches for clues to the mysterious circumstances surrounding his death, an investigation that forces her to confront her ethnicity and a family she never knew.
Includes bibliographical resources (p.).
ISBN 978-0-15-205507-3 (hardcover : alk. paper) 1. Chinese Americans—Juvenile fiction. [1. Chinese Americans—Fiction. 2. Identity—Fiction. 3. Journalism—Fiction. 4. Seattle (Wash.)—Fiction. 5. Mystery and detective stories.] I. Title.
PZ7.I533Pap 2010
[Fic]—dc22
2009023855

Manufactured in the United States of America
DOC 10 9 8 7 6 5 4 3 2 1

4500211906

For Troy James

A writer's job is to tell the truth, even when it is put into a story. Perhaps especially then.

This is the story of a boy—a man—called Fai-yi Li and of me, Margaret Wynn Chen, and of the true, hard things we learned because of each other.

I will tell you what I know of Fai-yi Li and leave him to tell you more if he chooses.

The important thing to understand about me is that I am Steven Chen's daughter, along with all that means.

CHAPTER 1

"Yours, Maggie." Mom pushed an envelope from the *Herald* down the counter where I was putting out bread for sandwiches.

I scanned the letter inside: "Now that school's out . . ."

"It's about things to bring on my first day," I told her.

"You're not still going?"

"I think so. I know it won't be the same—"

I broke off because Mom, who'd continued to sort through the mail, wasn't listening.

Unsettling doubt swept through me as I looked again at the letter from the newspaper, so businesslike, as though my summer internship were a real job. Which it was, of course, but this was written as though I were a regular employee instead of a high school student.

Mom, please! I wanted to say. *I'm kind of alone here!*

If Dad had still been there, he'd have said, *So you've got some paperwork to gather,* and then let me talk out my jitters one more time.

But Dad wasn't there. He never again would be, no matter how much I missed him and wanted him back. And whatever envelope Mom had just opened had triggered an annoyed "Humph."

With an effort, I smothered a twinge of resentment and focused on what she was saying. "Problem?" I asked.

She handed over a message printed on ivory-colored letterhead. "Please accept our condolences . . . However . . . Perhaps Mr. Chen attended a school with a similar name?"

"Must be a computer glitch," I said.

"And one more thing to take care of." The left corner of Mom's mouth twitched in a way it never had when Dad was alive.

A month earlier, in the days immediately after he died—no, not died, was killed by a hit-and-run driver—Mom had seemed so strong, moving from task to task. She'd notified old friends and dealt with police and lawyers.

But then she'd begun losing focus, becoming less and less able to separate the things that mattered from those that didn't. Fretting over small stuff and not remembering what was big.

Like my internship in the *Herald*'s newsroom. She'd even forgotten that, when it was the last thing Dad and I had planned together. I could understand, sort of. A summer job probably wasn't very important, considered against all the other changes in our lives. But still . . .

"As though I don't know perfectly well what prep school my husband attended."

"Don't worry about it," I told her. "If you want, I'll call next week and straighten things out."

"Things shouldn't need straightening out," she said. "They shouldn't have written as though one of their own students was some unknown person." Her face was drawn tight, its fine creases like the crackled lines of a glazed plate on the verge of breaking.

Dad would have known how to make her feel better. He always had known how to fix whatever needed fixing, whether it was a leaky faucet or a sad heart. But Dad couldn't make this trouble right, because his being gone *was* the trouble, for Mom and me both.

And we didn't have anyone else to help us, either. No family except for Mom's parents, scientists doing research half a world away. No close friends, because we hadn't lived in Seattle long enough to make any. Bett and Aimee, the girls I knew best, had left for summer places as soon as vacation started, and for Mom, the whole idea of allowing in anyone new was "Not yet, not now."

On impulse I said, "Let's skip the tuna sandwiches. We can go to a movie and out for pizza, after. Please?"

Mom shook her head, but then something—maybe my voice held an odd note I hadn't intended that said how much I needed things to be different—made her look at me the way she used to. The planes of her face briefly softened, as though she'd glimpsed that I was lonely and mixed-up. Scared and not certain of anything anymore. And although she hesitated, she finally said, "Sure. I'll be ready in half a shake."

Only she wasn't, and I searched both floors before finally finding her in the basement, peering into the washing machine.

"Mom, we've got to hurry if we want to make the early show."

"I thought I had time to run this," she said. "I don't know why the machine's filling so slowly."

Her focus was gone again, and she sounded as though we had no plans for the evening except to do laundry. Maybe because she didn't want to remember that the last time we had gone to a movie together, Dad had taken us.

"Come on," I said, putting my arm around her. "Let's watch

a chick flick he wouldn't have gone to in a million years. And we'll order anchovies on our pizza. For sure he wouldn't have eaten those!"

We saw a picture so bad it was perfect, and we came home still laughing—laughing hard for the first time since Dad had been around to laugh with us.

"Chocolate sundaes," Mom said. "That's what we need now. You want to make them while I move the laundry to the dryer?"

Then, moments later, voice panicky, she yelled, "Maggie!" She'd stopped partway down the basement stairs. Below her, water covered the floor.

"I'll cut the power," I said, and I ran to the electrical box in the garage.

With flashlights to guide us, we waded to the laundry room. Water gushed from a split washing machine hose. It stopped when we turned the valves off, but the mess!

By midnight, an outfit that specialized in cleanup emergencies had sucked the water away, sprayed mildew retardant, and provided fans to hurry the drying-out. The damage wasn't too bad, as most of the basement was unfinished.

Dad's office was the exception. There, studs were exposed where the cleanup crew had cut away the buckled bottoms of wallboard, and the flat-weave blue carpet, though it no longer squished when we stepped on it, was still damp.

But the worst thing about the room was that it was now empty. Dad's furniture had been moved out, and his stacks of loose papers and boxes of files had been carried upstairs to the kitchen, making it smell of wet cardboard and glue.

Dad's work *was* Dad, and for it to be gone, too . . .

How could we keep losing more and more of him? Would a day come when there'd be a final loss and then, *poof,* he'd be gone completely? The fact of him disappeared?

It took us a long two hours to take everything out to the garage for drying. By the time we were done, we had newspaper clippings dangling from wires stretched overhead, business papers spread on plastic sheets, and reporter's notebooks fanned out atop tools.

I began peeling Dad's favorite photo of us away from the wet glass of its frame. Dye in the ten-year-old brown matting had run, fingering rust across our black hair and splotching Mom's delicate features and my little-girl face, with my round cheeks and eyes full of questions.

"This must have been taken with our old film camera," I said. "Maybe we still have the negative."

I was just talking, trying to fill the damp, sad air, and I didn't expect Mom to answer. Her hands were clasped beneath her chin, squeezed tight, knuckles pale. She said, "I don't know how I'm going to sort all this out."

In recent days I'd seen Mom look stunned and seen her at a loss, seen her cry and seen her gather her will. Now, surrounded by broken cartons and soaked papers, with even the dry things in disordered piles, she sagged back, eyes closed. "I can't," she said. "I just can't."

Her words scared me because they expressed how I felt, too: like sagging back, giving up. Yet I was even more frightened by what would happen if we did give up.

So I said, "I can do some. I still have a week before I start my internship."

I went to my room dead tired but too wound up to sleep, and instead of trying to, I booted my computer and watched the *Herald*'s homepage pulse onto the screen. Shapes interlaced into columns of type, and headlines dissolved one into another. A photo of a migrant workers' camp became a picture of an immigration agent, which became images of a reporter asking, listening, writing. The display promised the kind of story my dad might have worked on, about real people with different views of what was needed and what was fair. The kind of story I could picture myself writing one day. All I had to do was squint to imagine that it was my photo on the screen, that I was the reporter stepping into an unfamiliar place and getting to know its truths.

I had an idea what that would mean, because I knew what newspapering had meant to Dad, whose news service stories had appeared in print and electronic media across the country. Along with Mom and me, Dad's work had been his life.

And I knew how proud he'd been that I wanted a news career, too.

When the *Herald* notified me that I'd been chosen to be one of the paper's high school interns, he'd been as excited as I was. Even at breakfast the next morning he kept talking about it, until he noticed the time.

"Whoa!" he exclaimed. "My plane!" And after a last gulp of coffee he grabbed his carry-on, gave us fast kisses, and headed out.

"Where's he off to this time?" I asked as Mom and I followed him outside.

"Boise, and then Spokane."

Dad, backing down the driveway, made the "okay" sign with his thumb and forefinger. *All's okay with the Chens.* Mom, waving back, made the sign, too, completing the ritual. *Yes, all's okay.*

I just waved, but then, suddenly, I ran barefoot to his car, motioning for the window to be opened. "Dad, what if I can't do the job?"

"You'll do fine," he said. "I guarantee it."

He backed a few feet more and then stopped again. And even though he had Seattle traffic to fight and the airport hassle to deal with, he spoke to me as though he had all the time in the world. "That answer wasn't fair," he said. "I can't guarantee anything, but I can tell you what I believe. And that's that you're going to be the best intern the *Herald* has ever hired."

I nodded, understanding that he wouldn't have been Dad if he'd let even the best-meant half-truth go uncorrected. But my question needed fixing, too. "The thing is," I said, "what if I don't like working there? Don't like the news? When journalism is all I've ever thought about doing?"

"Then you'll have learned something about yourself while all the choices are still in front of you."

It briefly looked as if a shadow crossed Dad's face, though there wasn't enough sunlight leaking through the overcast sky to make one. And anyway, in another instant the corners of his eyes crinkled and his voice held laughter. "And as for the news business being your only ambition—I seem to recall plans to be just like your kindergarten teacher, and an earlier ambition to raise elephants."

"Giraffes," I corrected.

"Giraffes, then. Maggie, the point is, you don't have to decide, at sixteen, what you want to be for the rest of your life. Or who."

"What do you mean, *who?*" I asked, because the word didn't seem to exactly follow, and another thing that defined Dad was the logical way his mind worked. But by then he was looking at his watch, and I didn't get an answer.

I never saw my father again. A few days after that, driving home from Sea-Tac Airport, he stopped at a convenience store, and as he was getting out of his car, another car hit him.

And now the dad who had been part of every day of my life was gone.

CHAPTER 2

I didn't get to the sorting right away. Mom worked at a local college, filling in for an English professor on maternity leave, so I was the one who had to be around for the insurance company agent, the plumber, the drywaller, and the carpet store man. And then see them again when they returned with estimates for repairing the basement damage.

The drywaller had just left on Tuesday afternoon when Mom phoned to say she needed to stay at school for an evening reading and reception for an author.

"No problem," I told her. "I can get myself something to eat."

Our old dog, Pepper, followed me to the kitchen, her body wiggling with pleasure and her nose nudging me to the treat jar. I rubbed behind her ears and measured out her dinner instead. And then I put cold cuts on a cheese bagel and took it out to the garage.

In the couple of days since the water disaster, I'd put off looking in here, and now I took a step back from the mess of stuff hanging down, laid out, and stacked up on all sides. Where was I ever going to start?

I leafed through a file folder of utility and phone bills, each marked with the date Dad had paid them. The ones on the bottom were still damp, so I turned the pile over and spread it out. Then I did the same with a couple of other files that were also in need of additional drying.

Oh, Dad, do we really need to keep all this? I thought, as though he might actually answer.

Sometimes it still didn't seem quite real that he was gone, any more than it had the night we heard.

It had been a Friday. I'd stayed late with rest of the journalism club, getting out the school newspaper, and afterward we'd gone for ice cream. Racing the evening chill, I'd hurried into the house calling ahead, "Mom! I'm home, and . . ."

My words had trailed off when I caught sight of her standing by a living-room window, talking on her cell phone. It was how *still* she stood that stopped me. How motionless her body and how quiet her face.

"I see," she said. "No, I understand."

I watched, then moved closer. "What's wrong?" I whispered. I asked, "Is it Dad?" although I already knew because of how Mom was looking at me.

After the call she held me for a long time, so tight, before telling me *what* and *when,* and she kept holding me while I tried to understand.

But then, and even now, what I couldn't quite fit my mind around was the time gap between Dad's dying, which had been in the afternoon, and my learning of it that night. For those few hours, even though he'd been physically dead, he continued to be alive to me because I didn't know any different. And so, I sometimes thought, if I'd never found out otherwise . . .

But of course, I had.

Earlier that day two policemen had come to tell Mom what had happened. Even before notifying her, they called the news agency bureau where Dad worked, and it was his boss who had identified Dad's body and who was talking to Mom when I got home.

The next morning, I'd searched through the newspaper to learn more, but I didn't. I had to hunt even to find the story at all, bypassing headlines about an airline strike, school budgets, a drive-by shooting. Finally, on an inside page with other late-breaking news, I'd found just one paragraph. "Respected journalist Steven Chen was the victim . . ."

Blinking back the tears that always welled up when I remembered that night, I pulled a dry clipping off the line. *Maybe,* I thought, *I should start a keeper pile.* I decided to put things we'd definitely want to save in one place, where they couldn't get thrown away by accident.

Such as this clipping, an article not by Dad but about him: a story about the last big journalism award he'd gotten. Of all the awards he'd received, it was the most important to him, and Mom and I had gone to the banquet where he'd received it. He'd worn a tux, and we'd worn new dresses.

The picture above the story showed the three of us, and even without reading the caption, people would know we were a family—it was the way we stood with no space between us and how similar we looked, Dad and me especially. A Chinese family, they might think, not realizing that our China-born ancestors on both sides were more generations back than we knew.

Now, looking at our smiles in that press photo, I remembered how proud I'd been listening to the presenter's speech. "Steven Chen is a reporter's reporter," she'd said. "He writes the truth honestly, without omission or slant."

Mainly because of that award, the news agency that Dad

wrote for had offered him a transfer to New York and a national/international beat. He surprised everyone by choosing to come here instead, to cover regional business news. He didn't give much of a reason—just, "The Northwest is growing in importance. It's a good spot for a newshound."

And since neither Mom nor I had wanted to move to New York, we hadn't asked for more. Though after he got killed, Mom, over breakfast one day, had suddenly exclaimed, "Who'd have thought Manhattan might be safer than Seattle?"

I hadn't answered her then, but I did now, aloud, in the glue-smelling, paper-webbed, memory-tangled lonely mess of a garage. "No one. No one!" No one would have thought it, and what happened wasn't right, and I didn't know what to do with this clipping or with all the stuff that was still wet, or with the way I felt . . .

How I wished I had someone to talk to and work with. A brother or a sister. Perhaps a big family. Aunts to chatter and keep everyone fed and uncles to string more drying wires and help with bundling cardboard for recycling.

Or even a friend. If Bett and Aimee weren't fifty miles away in the San Juan Islands, I might have called them to come over. But they were.

So I put the award banquet story safely back on the line, and then found and rearranged several items that were still damp.

It was Thursday by the time all the things we'd taken up from Dad's office were completely dry. I was mentally dividing the garage into areas for a preliminary sort when Mom came out to tell me she was on her way to work.

"I hate leaving you with all this," she said.

"I've got a plan. And the work will keep my mind off starting at the *Herald* next week. I'm ready to admit I'm getting nervous."

"Not too late to change your mind. Whoever's running the intern program probably chose alternates."

"No," I said. "I want to do it. I just want to do it *well.* If I don't, I'll embarrass myself, you, and the teachers who wrote me recommendations."

"Maggie!" she exclaimed. Sudden, laughing exasperation made her sound like her old self. "You'll do fine! You're your father's daughter. You've got printer's ink in your veins!"

I held my breath, waiting for the wipeout I was sure would follow when Mom's mirth collapsed atop memories. But this time it didn't. She gave me a hug. "You'll do yourself, me, and your teachers proud. Which reminds me. Did you call your father's prep school?"

For a moment I didn't know what she was talking about. Then I remembered the letter saying he wasn't on its alumni list. Even though Dad hadn't kept up with associations there, Mom wanted the school to know he'd died.

"Not yet," I said. "I'll do it today. I promise."

Once Mom was gone, I began a rough triage, identifying papers as *toss, keep,* or *decide later.*

At first I worked quickly, but pretty soon my scanning became reading. I stopped to study the draft of one of Dad's columns. His published articles had always been so smooth and seemed so effortless that the draft surprised me, with its arrows and inserted words and cross-outs over cross-outs.

Then I began reading his reporter's notebooks, which I went through as I picked them up. Some were from twenty years earlier, others quite recent, and the images they brought to mind made me feel a bittersweet ache. And a swelling pride, too. This was the dad I knew, but more, also. Someone connected to the world in a thousand ways and able, through his writing, to let others know what that was like.

Dad hadn't recorded just what he saw as he went after a story; he also got the sound and smell and feel, sometimes even the taste of it. Quoted words got a context and often a reminder of how they were said. "Shouted over the scream of machinery . . ." "Whispered, as her eyes searched the deserted street . . ."

I smiled at the way, in between notes such as those, he'd jotted down personal reminders like "Pick up the turkey"—that would have been Thanksgiving two years past—and research questions: "Federal law in effect when? Any changes?"

And he'd tracked ongoing projects: the effects of a factory closure, tourism trends, a business forecast. In a notebook so new the last pages were blank, he'd written, "Progress on family project, finally? Possible search will end right here! Give mail a week, then fly CA."

It sounded like a story he'd worked on for a good while, but I didn't recall him mentioning it. Often, at dinner, he did talk about his work.

I thought he must have received whatever he was looking for, since I was pretty sure he hadn't made any recent trips to California.

I flipped to the next page, but the only thing on it was a note. "The trouble with small deceits is that the poet was right: they do become tangled webs. And you can't foresee who will become ensnared in them or who will be hurt if you tear back through to the truth."

I felt guilty reading thoughts that Dad had obviously written only for himself. It was crossing a line of privacy I'd never have crossed when he was alive. But I told myself that maybe he'd have wanted me to read his notes now. They were probably the last things I'd ever learn directly from him. Things and ideas that maybe he'd intended to tell me about one day.

Or explain. Obviously Dad was thinking about some lie someone had told when he wrote that last entry. I thought there was probably a story there I'd have enjoyed hearing.

CHAPTER 3

I didn't take a break till noon, when I put a frozen lunch in the microwave and set about keeping my promise to call Dad's school.

Intending to get the number from the school's website, I turned on the computer Mom kept in the kitchen, and while it was starting up, I brought in the mail.

A postcard from the national headquarters of Dad's college fraternity fell out. It was a form for reporting address changes, but someone had written on it, "No Steven Chen in our records."

This was absurd, I thought. How could two places Dad had been a part of both have lost track of him?

The microwave beeped that my lunch was done, but I ignored it and called the prep school instead. A recorded message said that the office was closed for summer maintenance, but in case of emergencies . . .

So I called Columbia University and asked to be connected to Dad's fraternity house.

"We have no listing for that," a campus operator told me.

"But you must," I said. "My dad was a member."

"Are you sure you have the fraternity name right? My own kid calls himself a Delt, when really the proper designation is—"

"I think I do," I said, "but I could check. Is there someone who would look up my father's records for me?"

She referred me to an online website where I meandered around, followed outside links, and never did learn anything. The only reason I gave it any time at all was that the fraternity mix-up, coming on top of the letter from the prep school, created a puzzle that nagged at me.

Finally I dug through sympathy cards looking for one from a Bill Ames, who'd written that he was a college friend of Dad's and had seen the obituary. Using his return address to get a home phone number, I called and heard my call being forwarded to his cell.

When he answered, I explained the trouble I was having connecting with Dad's old fraternity. "I thought perhaps you might have been in it with him."

He didn't reply, so I said, "You did go to Columbia with my father?"

"Certainly," he said. "Though after we got our degrees, I didn't stay on for graduate work the way he did, going into journalism."

"But the fraternity?" I said.

"We weren't in one. The two of us worked together on a cafeteria steam line."

"Maybe you're thinking of another friend," I said. "I don't think Dad had a job while he was in college."

"Sure he did. Work-study, like me. Plus, Steven held down outside jobs. He had to, being on his own."

I disconnected, aware of a gnawing anxiousness, even though I knew Mr. Ames must have confused my dad with someone else.

Dad's parents hadn't been rich, but they'd had enough money

to put him through one of the priciest prep schools in the country and then through an Ivy League university.

Dad hadn't been comfortable talking about how well off they'd been—probably, I'd always thought, because he didn't want me thinking money was what counted. But Mom had told me how his parents, who'd died while Dad was in college, had set aside enough for his schooling and then left the rest to the natural history museum where they'd served as directors.

She liked to tell that part because the same museum had once funded some of her own parents' research, and she always said, with a coincidence like that, how could she and Dad *not* have ended up together?

So, no, there was no way my dad had had to work his way through school.

I knew that, yet I made one more call.

This time I telephoned the museum to ask about my grandparents. The man in charge of the museum's foundation was very nice on the phone. And very certain.

"Yes, the Chens were active with the museum for many years," he told me. "But," he went on, "they died in the 1970s, quite elderly and without any children or grandchildren." He knew that positively.

No children. No grandchildren. I thought of another possibility. "Perhaps there was some other couple by the name of Chen on your board of directors?"

"Possibly, before my time," he said, but then, after checking, he told me, "No. I've looked all the way back to when the museum was built."

I hung up, feeling as though I'd been yanked upside down

and that everything that should be steady and familiar was now swinging by, blurry and weird.

Arms crossed tightly, I fought for control. A turmoil of questions and answers raced across my mind.

Why? Why would my father, who'd always said a person was only as good as his or her word, have lied about his parents and about how he'd been brought up?

I couldn't come up with an explanation that would make his lie be all right. In fact, I couldn't think of one that I could even believe.

He made up a story because he was ashamed of the truth? I couldn't imagine it.

Because he wanted a background that would help him fit in with the business world he wrote about? That seemed even less like him.

Again, I tried to tell myself I'd stumbled onto a trail of mistakes. The prep school, Columbia, Mr. Ames, the museum man—I wanted so much for them all to be wrong.

Yet along with learning not to lie to others, I'd grown up being taught not to lie to myself. Dad had been particularly big on that.

"Don't ever deny what you know," he once told me. He'd been talking about a business that had gone bankrupt because its owner had closed his eyes to problems he hadn't wanted to see. But Dad had made the point seem personal, a lesson for me. I shouldn't ever refuse to look at the truth.

And eventually a truth that I couldn't ignore emerged from my circling thoughts. Dad had never adequately explained his decision to bring us to Seattle, and now I had a reason. The move made sense if it had nothing to do with coming here and everything to do with avoiding New York and the East Coast, where he'd be closer to a phony background. Where he'd be at more risk for his lies being discovered.

I stayed by the phone a long time, thinking. I turned around and around the heirloom jade ring Dad had given me one Christmas, saying it was to remind me to be proud of who I was. Was it just a stage prop, bought from some jeweler who sold antique pieces?

I didn't care what family Dad came from. And I cared even less whether he came from a ton of money or from no money at all.

I just wanted him to have been honest about it.

Then another idea occurred to me. Maybe Dad didn't *know* where he came from. Didn't know *who* he came from.

That last morning, he told me I didn't have to decide, at sixteen years old, who I'd be the rest of my life.

Is that what he'd done? At some point, did he pick who he'd be? Because he didn't know?

I remembered the notebook entries I'd read just that morning, and I went out to the garage and read them again.

"Progress on family project, finally? Possible search . . ."

What if that didn't refer to a story Dad had been working on, but was about looking for the unknown persons who were his own family? What if he'd started a search to find out who he was, but had kept it to himself? Maybe he'd wanted to tell Mom and me, but hadn't known how.

That would explain the next entry, about lies leading to tangled webs and hurting people. Because if what I'd learned from my phone calls was true—and if the truth was that the most basic stuff Mom and I had always believed was really false—

I broke off, ensnared by my own web of illogic.

I was holding myself so rigidly my stomach muscles hurt. I felt angry and mixed-up. Off kilter. Felt, most of all, betrayed.

Nobody likes to be lied to, not by strangers trying to sell things or by casual friends making excuses for promises not kept. But lies like those are part of life. You guard against them, and if you get taken in anyway, the person you're most annoyed with is yourself.

Which is different from when you're taken in by a lie told by somebody you trust one hundred percent.

And it's especially different when that somebody is your father and the lie is so huge you can hardly comprehend the questions it raises.

I huddled on the garage floor, arms around my legs, chin on my knees, not able to get past the two biggest ones.

First: If Dad wasn't who he'd always said, then who was he?

And second: Who did that make me?

The harder I concentrated, the more blank my mind seemed to go. And then, somehow, the questions shifted just enough that I finally came up with sort of an answer. It didn't matter about Dad. I didn't need to be anyone other than who I'd always been.

Really, nothing had changed except that I'd made a few phone calls and learned a few things I didn't want to know. Things I could choose to forget.

I wouldn't even have to tell my mother. When she asked how my call to Dad's school had gone, I could tell her the school records were correct now, which would be the absolute truth.

Qualms fluttered through me—an inkling that forgetting

might not be that easy, a twinge of guilt that maybe I owed my father more.

But I flooded out the qualms with a sudden, flat-out rage.

It wasn't right for Dad to have built our family on a lie. It was selfish and mean, and I hated him for all the hurt I was feeling. And I wished he were there with me so I could tell him. So I could yell every mean thing I could think of and hurt him more than he'd hurt me.

Well, he'd got one thing right, anyway. Telling me I didn't have to decide right now who I'd be for the rest of my life. That meant that I *could* decide, if I wanted to.

I shoved the jade ring into a pocket of my jeans, and I ripped every page from the notebook. Then I tore the pages and even the notebook cover into shreds, which I buried deep in the trash.

I'd made my decision. I would be just exactly who I'd always been.

FAI-YI LI

The old man waited at the door for his sister, listening to the sound of her walker on the pavement. "What took you so long?" he asked.

"Lines at the stores," she said. "If you shopped, you would know."

"Was someone just here? I heard a car."

"No." She pushed by, threatening his balance. "Go sit. You are in my way."

He opened the living-room blinds to let in the afternoon sun, although he knew she would soon close them. The brightness created orange-veined patterns on the insides of his eyelids, as jagged as the remembered pictures he often saw and as branched as the words that went with them.

More and more often these days, he lived in those scenes.

SEATTLE, 1932

"What is your name?"

"Li Fai-yi," I answer.

"We do not believe you."

"Li Fai-yi." The name comes strangely to my tongue, stranger still to my mind. But I have to remember. That is who I must say I am.

"And your sister's?"

"Li Sucheng."

Two men sit across a table from me. One asks questions in words I do not understand, and the other puts them into my language so that I will. He does not say why he sometimes turns the names around, Fai-yi Li, Sucheng Li, putting the family name last.

"And your age?"

"Fifteen. We are both fifteen. Twins."

"And why do you wish to be admitted to the United States?"

"To be with our father, Li Dewei." I wonder if I should give other reasons also. To work. To go to school. I cannot tell them, To keep Sucheng from being arrested.

"You say he is your father. How do we know?"

"There are papers. You have papers from him. Please look."

The man in charge flicks through a file. His stomach growls, and he mutters to the other man, the bad-smelling one who translates. "We're going for lunch. Wait here, boy."

So I wait alone in the small room, sitting straight-backed, elbows in, at the scarred white table. My own stomach growls, sounding loud over the muffled, crying-out, calling-sharp, despairing, ordering, submitting, many-languaged voices coming from the other side of the thin wall.

I wonder if I will ever again know days when no one is a stranger, no word unknown, when the next moment is predictable and unthreatening. I know I must remain alert, but I am so tired from struggling to understand the men's questions.

How long will they be gone? I should be remembering what I have said, so that I will say it exactly the same way again, but my mind separates from my will, roving across real pictures instead of the ones I have memorized.

I see the village where my sister and I and our parents and grandparents were born. A place where one did not have to look very far back to find one life becoming another, or dream very far forward to find life stretching out that way. Only along the sides of a person's life were there fixed boundaries, and beyond them an unknown of half-believed tales.

I think of how one night I sat apart, smelling the food my mother and sister were cooking, trying to understand the laughter of men talking about crops and weather and politics and people. A second cousin from the city told of planning to go to America, which he called the Gold Mountain. There, he said, there was so much wealth—gold for the picking up—that nothing else mattered.

"Gold will not keep you warm at night," a neighbor said. "I hear there are few Chinese women in America."

"After I am rich, I will bring over a wife to rub my back when it aches from bending over to gather the nuggets," the cousin says. "Perhaps Sucheng there."

This caused more laughter, for it was well known my beautiful twin thought much of herself.

"And how will you get there to begin with?" asked my father.

"I will pay a Gold Mountain firm to arrange that," the cousin replied. "Those firms know more ways to slip past laws than a cat by a lazy dog."

"And you have this money?"

"No. That is why I am only planning!" The cousin laughed as hard as the others.

Afterward I asked my father why it was funny that the cousin wanted to go someplace he could not.

"Because he knows he'll never have to test his dreams," my father said. "There's no place on earth where gold erupts like boulders in a frost heave."

"The teacher's family lives well on money a son in America sends back," I argued.

"Not that well," my father said. "If riches were free for the taking, the son would send more."

I glimpsed Sucheng's face above the dishpan. She wanted to believe that the cities our cousin had spoken of had golden streets, just as she wanted to believe she would do more than marry a village man and live out the life that was before her.

It was the difference between us. I did not wish to be anyone but who I was.

‘ ‘ ‘

The door opens. A man looks in and then goes away. It is another tiny piece added to my bewilderment.

The officials at this reception center do no explaining. They order you, "In this line. Open your bag. Bend your head." They mean now, *and they do not tell you why you are to do a thing or what you will be told to do next. But you know you must do it right.*

I wonder if Sucheng is being interrogated also, and if she will remember to say it is forty-three steps from our house to the privy. She was not as good as I at learning the details to prove we are Li Dewei's children. But perhaps they will not think a girl worth questioning.

‘ ‘ ‘

My thoughts drift back into memories, and now, not such good ones. Soon after that evening of laughter I was sent to relatives to be safe from a sickness moving through our village, while Sucheng was kept at home to help our parents, who did not want to leave their store. When I returned, her face was no longer as smooth as porcelain but pocked like lava rock, and her bitterness pervaded every corner of our house.

And then came another evening and another visitor, a worn-looking, thin stranger whose bony shoulders carried hardness and need, and again, Sucheng and I listened to men's talk. We heard the man speak of a wife who had died and of children who needed care.

Afterward she whispered in a choked fury of impotence, "I won't go with such a poor person. I'll run away first."

I knew it for an empty threat, for where could she go? "Perhaps he is better off than he seems," I said.

With an impatient chop of her hand, she dismissed that. "If he could afford better, he wouldn't want to marry me."

"I am sorry," I said, for I had no other answer to give.

‘ ‘ ‘

Two nights later, just past moonrise, I watched blood from a scalp wound seep into rocky earth. It came from the stranger's sprawled body, half hidden under Sucheng's small jacket.

Terrified, she flung incoherent words at me. "I didn't mean . . . I didn't recognize him. He attacked . . . I only pushed, and he fell. Fai-yi, you have to believe me! You do?"

"Of course," I answered as I struggled to think clearly.

"But what if no one else does? What if people say I killed him on purpose so I would not have to go with him?"

"They will not," I told her, though even to myself I sounded unconvincing. The village might well think Sucheng would murder rather than be hauled off to be field hand, cook, and servant to someone else's children.

"But if they do, if I'm arrested, I might be killed."

She huddled close, the way she did when we were little and thunderstorms or Father's anger or a snake in a grain bag frightened her. "Fai-yi, I don't want to be put to death. Take me away."

"Where to?" My eyes searched the dark, familiar wooded path as though a branch to a new place might suddenly appear. "There's nowhere that we wouldn't eventually be found."

Her toe nudged the jacket covering the gaping gash in the man's head. The bloody, pointed rock that he must have fallen on lay nearby. "There's the Gold Mountain."

I stared at her. "We don't know anything about America, or how to get there."

"There are those firms that arrange things."

"For money. We don't have any."

"He might," she said. Her foot pushed aside the jacket. "He was going to pay for me. Check his pockets."

When I refused, she checked them herself, and she found a good amount. Not wealth, but far more than I'd have expected, though what did I know of such things?

"That money is not ours," I protested.

"He no longer needs it."

"His family will."

"And if they don't get this money, will anyone go after them and execute them for a crime they didn't commit?"

"It's stealing."

She thrust her face in front of mine, forcing me to see how moonlight caught on welts and cast shadows into the pits of her skin. "And nobody stole from me? What if you'd been the one kept home?"

I heard the anger behind her fear, and the pain beyond that. I had known my twin's one-time hopes as though they were mine, and our parents had recognized them also. They, too, had known that there might be more possible for Sucheng than for a girl less lovely, and still they had risked her and not me.

"Sucheng," I said, "they could not know you would get the sickness."

Abruptly, she reached for the dead man. "Take his legs!" she ordered. "We must move him out of sight."

Looking back now, I think that is where I went wrong. I should have refused. But her urgency was so great that I obeyed without thinking. Across the body, we kept arguing. We argued about our chances of getting away. About whether Gold Mountain firms really existed. About what was the right thing to do.

"Right!" Sucheng exploded. "My brother, you owe me this!"

· · ·

Hiding and fearful, we traveled on foot to the city, where we slept as we could and ate sparingly during the time it took us to find one of those firms that arranged passages overseas.

"You don't just go to America," the firm's agent told us. "Not unless you're someone wanted, like a teacher. However," he went on, "if a person there, a citizen, were willing to claim you as his children . . ."

"We don't know anyone," I said.

The man asked how much money we could spend to find someone.

Holding back only a little, I showed him. He grumbled that it was hardly enough for his firm's work, for our passage, for some stranger who would certainly not help us for free, but, perhaps . . .

And eventually, after many more days of hiding, Sucheng and I were told of Li Dewei of Seattle, in the United States.

"Your new father!" the agent said, shoving papers at me. "You can read? You and your sister must learn all this so you will know how he came to have children born in China."

I taught the story to Sucheng, and on the ship to America we practiced it. We had been warned: "One mistake, say one thing different than what you should say, and you'll be sent back." And so we practiced the story every day, over and over.

But at night I lay awake thinking about what we had done. Had I been right to give in to Sucheng? Had her need to escape really been as desperate as it seemed that night we fled? Did one deception have to follow another, as they had since that first decision to help her hide the dead man?

And how long would it be, I wondered, before I could return to China?

Then finally, this morning, we reached land, and through a sleety fog I watched my sister being taken off with the other women.

* * *

The door opens again. It is the men returning to question me more, and this time their questions are different. They begin, "It was reported . . ." and "We've been told you are wanted!"

They say, "Tell us about the crime."

My heart beats fast and the room spins. How do they know?

"We're going to put you on the next ship, in the hold with the rats and foul seepage. That is what we do with criminals. Tell us. How much money did you steal? Show us. Show us."

In terror, I put on the table all the money that I have left. It is Chinese currency, and the man who translates counts it and then talks to the other.

Then he says to me, "You are fortunate. We have decided it was someone else who is wanted."

A mark is made on their paper, like a drawing—"S/N"—and I am told, "Enough. You are believed. You may go."

"Go . . . ?"

I am not sure what they mean.

"To the Gold Mountain," I am told, and the two men laugh and laugh. And then I understand that they know nothing at all except their own power.

I leave without the money I put on the table, but I now have an identification paper that I must keep with me. It says I am Fai-yi Li.

CHAPTER 4

I wanted to stay white-hot angry. As long as fury filled the new, empty space at the edges of everywhere, I didn't have to think about the unknown person my father had become.

And I wanted my mother to feel it with me. She'd been wronged as much as I had. Maybe more. She'd been Dad's wife. He'd lied to her.

Time after time through the weekend I came so close to telling Mom all I'd learned.

But always, I stopped myself. Once I told the secret, I wouldn't be able to untell it.

Besides, hurting her wouldn't make me hurt less. It would only increase the pain already cloaking her like a curtain between us. Maybe knowing would be the final weight that would pull her under and drown her. Then I would have two parents who were all the way lost.

So I kept my anger in and let it morph into the dull ache I felt when I thought of Dad. An ache that I was mostly able to hide.

Sunday, though, a small line furrowed Mom's forehead, and she asked if there was something I wanted to talk about.

I lied. "Not a thing," I said.

It was early evening, and she was about to leave for dinner.

"I can stay home with you," she said. "It's just a few of the women faculty getting together. They won't miss me."

"No. I'm glad you're finally getting out." I gave her a phony grin. "I've got big plans of my own. I'm going to take a long bath, do my nails, talk to Bett and Aimee, and watch TV."

"You're not still nervous about starting work tomorrow?"

I lied again. "Nope. Got it under control."

I waved from the window as Mom pulled away. I'd been right, not telling her about Dad's deceit. It was best for her and for me, too. Or I was sure it would be, eventually.

I just wished I could understand.

I fixed a sandwich and ate it. I picked up the phone and put it back down. I went into the bathroom, filled the tub, and half undressed. And then I put my T-shirt and shorts back on and slipped into sandals.

"I cannot stay in this house another minute," I told Pepper.

I felt wired, as though a low dose of adrenaline was circuiting through me. Perhaps it was letdown from working so hard sorting Dad's things and then having the work suddenly done. Mom and I had finished that afternoon.

Or perhaps, despite what I'd told Mom, it was apprehension over starting at the *Herald*.

Or maybe I was restless because the sudden free hours had caught me unawares and allowed feelings that I'd been smothering now to bubble up.

With Pepper in the back seat of the used Civic Mom and Dad bought me when we moved to Seattle, I began driving east, not heading anyplace in particular. I wanted the calm of not thinking, and if I couldn't have that, I wanted to put the past from my mind and focus my thoughts on what lay in front of me.

Soon, though, lights outlining the edge of Lake Washington came into view, and they reminded me of the March evening just a few months earlier when Mom and Dad and I had first explored our new city. "A city defined by water," I remembered Mom murmuring.

I turned back and started a long, looping tour around Seattle. Now, as then, yellowed squares on the University of Washington campus broke the falling darkness, and the downtown skyline was silhouetted against its own glow. *So many people, living so many different lives,* I thought. Private lives, unless they did something to make them public—ran for office, won a lottery, did something wrong. Which was where reporters came in, and papers and news broadcasts. Where digging for the truth began.

Dad was the one who'd taught me to always be aware that things might not be as they appear.

On the far side of the city I turned south and drove along the wharf area, where halogen lamps lighted huge cargo cranes unloading ships.

Overall, Seattle was a pretty hard place to get lost in: just a narrow strip with Lake Washington on the east and Puget Sound on the west. It was navigating the every-which-way, older streets that could get confusing.

The way they must have for Dad, that day when he was on

his way home from the airport. The accident had happened near the International District. Police figured that Dad must have tried to avoid a traffic jam by exiting I-5 early and then gotten lost after leaving the area that used to be known as Chinatown. They guessed he'd parked in front of the convenience store because he intended to ask for directions.

For Dad, I thought, *who was such a traveler, to get lost so close to home . . .*

Stopped at a traffic light, I looked across the water to the far-off distance where the Olympic Mountains pierced a dimly luminous charcoal sky. I could imagine the Pacific Ocean beyond them.

Mom and Dad had taken me to the ocean more than once over the years, to keep up a tradition of birthday celebrations that had begun when I was five and my favorite picture book was *Harry by the Sea.* We were living in Nevada then, but we'd driven all the way to the California coast just so I could put my feet into a real sea that went so far it was hard to imagine its end.

My dad had made sure I understood that there *was* an end to the Pacific, though, where it merged into new oceans and crashed onto the shores of different lands. In fact, he'd said, if we got into a boat and sailed sure and straight, we'd wind up in China, where I'd look so much like everyone else that I'd blend right into the woodwork.

"Why would I want to do that?" I'd asked, making him and Mom laugh.

He'd answered, "Blending in can be handy. And as for sailing beyond what you can see? *Beyond* is where you find the best surprises. Beyond into the unknown."

Now I wondered if perhaps Dad's unknown family might be over there, in China. But then I remembered the notebook entry about how his search might end right here in Seattle.

We'd driven home from that first ocean trip the same night so that Dad could catch a plane the next morning. Even by then he was more than a local reporter. And along the way, as we crossed a silver-tipped desert, he'd taught me a rhyme to remember when I missed him. "I see the moon and the moon sees me. The moon sees someone I want to see."

A horn sounded behind me, and I realized the light had turned. I started forward, waving an apology.

"The moon sees someone I want to see." I whispered the words, letting myself miss Dad for the first time since I learned of his deceit. And for the first time, too, I felt a little sorry for him. It must have been hard not knowing where he came from. Wondering if he had, somewhere, a whole family he didn't know.

He'd have felt a void. I knew because I felt it in me. The part of me that had been the story family Dad made up was gone, and I had nothing—nobody and no real story—to replace it.

Perhaps I'd been too hasty, destroying his notebook. Maybe further on, after the notes I'd read, there were other notes that would have pointed me to whoever my unknown blood relatives might be. Not that I'd necessarily want to meet them. But if I just knew who they were . . .

But I had destroyed it, and anyway, to the best of my memory, the remaining pages had been blank.

I drove the rest of the way home, considering whether I should pick up the search where Dad left off. *Could I?* I wouldn't have to make a big deal of it, just maybe gather a little information. I certainly wouldn't tell my mother what I was doing. And I'd keep my focus on the important thing in front of me—my internship.

But there was Mr. Ames. Working together, he and Dad must have talked. Maybe one day soon I'd give him another call.

CHAPTER 5

I really should have figured out my clothes before going to bed on Sunday night, but I didn't, so I began Monday morning pulling things from my closet. Most of my wardrobe consisted of jeans and T-shirts. One long dress, worn to the spring prom with a senior I didn't particularly want to see again. Some shorts, two skirts, and one pair of natural linen pants that I hated because of the way they wrinkled.

In other words, I didn't own anything fit for going to work.

I borrowed a cream-colored shirt from Mom, put it on with the linen pants, and then, studying myself in the mirror, debated whether I should go with jeans and a pullover instead. I didn't want to look like a kid playing dress-up. But I didn't want to look like just a kid, either.

Half an hour later, wearing Mom's top and the good pants, I stood in the *Herald*'s lobby waiting for the receptionist to complete a phone call. Beyond her desk, the cavernous newsroom stretched out, electronic air humming and fluorescent lights buzzing.

Screen savers floated across computer screens on unoccupied desks, and the people who were there visited quietly or leaned back in their chairs reading newspapers. A silent television tuned to CNN went unwatched.

My insides fluttered with nervous excitement. I'd imagined myself in a place like this even before I could picture it. All the way back in preschool, when other kids played fireman and store, I'd handed out scribbled pages that I said was my newspaper. And now, now this was a real newsroom, and I belonged in it. Or I had a chance to belong, anyway. *If I can just, please, get off to a good start.*

The peaceful scene continued unchanged for a moment more. Then a radio squawked, a man called, "I'm on it!" and the lull broke into movement and sound.

Behind me the outside doors opened, and a girl about my age swept in along with a blast of fresh, humid air. It twined her gauzy skirt and lifted her frizzy red curls. Not pausing in the lobby, she continued her whirlwind flurry past me and into the newsroom itself.

The startled receptionist put down the phone, called, "Wait!" and brought her back. She got our names straight—Margaret Chen, Jillian Smythe—and ordered, "Stay here. I'll let someone know our interns have arrived."

"Blew that, didn't I?" the girl said, laughing as she dropped into a chair. Her gaze roved the newsroom the way mine had. She didn't act embarrassed, and only a slight pink color seeping up her neck gave away that she was. If it had been me being hauled back from a mistake first thing, I'd have been mortified.

She turned to me with a quick appraising glance. "So, Margaret, I thought you'd be a boy," she said. "For gender balance. But I suppose you're brainy?"

"No! Or—" How was I supposed to answer? Tell her my IQ, which I didn't know? I settled for saying, "Actually, I go by Maggie."

But she was already done with me and on her feet, not quite launching herself into the newsroom again, but close to it. The receptionist, back on the phone, pressed her lips together and shot me a disapproving glance, as though I were responsible for Jillian.

I folded my arms, realized how defensive that looked, and unfolded them.

Probably Jillian had not dithered one minute over what to wear, hadn't worried at all whether she needed to appear older or younger or be anyone different from who she was.

A long ten minutes later a tall woman with careful makeup and clicking heels crossed to us from a wide stairway on the other side of the lobby. Catching a nod from the receptionist, she said, "Girls? Want to come down to Personnel? I've got some paperwork for you."

She went over the forms and then deposited Jillian and me in a small conference room. "Take your time filling them out. When you're done, I'll let the newsroom know you're ready to go to work."

"So," Jillian said as soon as we were alone, "I wondered who the other intern would be. Like I said, I figured it would be a guy, for balance. But"—she gave me a sideways glance—"maybe they needed an ethnic pick more?"

I shot her a disbelieving look, stunned she'd say that, even if she did think it, and I had no idea how to tell her all the ways she'd been rude.

"Right. American," I finally answered, and picked up the top page.

I printed my name and other easy stuff in the boxes of an income tax withholding form and put down zero for the number of dependents I wished to claim.

Jillian said, "You ought to at least count yourself." Then she watched while I declined health insurance, which Mom had said I didn't need.

"Do you mind?" I said, leaning away.

"Mind what?" she asked, leaning with me. Then, "Oh! Am I being nosy? Sorry, but that does go with being at a

newspaper, doesn't it? I mean, there are so few careers where you can get paid for poking into other people's business, and some of them you can get killed doing, like if you're a CIA agent."

I had no idea if she was serious, though I thought probably not. If she was as ditsy as she sounded, the *Herald* would never have hired her.

I moved on to a form for emergency contact information.

"Although," she went on, "it's not like people can get away with many real secrets anymore. Like, one time, *one time,* I cut school, and who do you think showed up on YouTube? *Moi.* And you know that thing about five degrees of separation?"

"Six," I said. "It's six degrees."

"Six would be bad enough. But the point is, it was YouTube, then my mom's boss's daughter's computer. Him. Mom. Me, grounded. So—"

She broke off to read what I'd just put down. "Only your mom for a contact?" she asked. "Divorced, or you just have no dad, period?"

I said I needed more working room and moved to another chair.

"Oh!" she said. "Sure. All you had to say was you didn't want to talk."

I'd expected that Fran Paglioni, the Metro editor in charge of the high school intern program, would get us started in our jobs, but Mr. Braden, the *Herald*'s editor in chief, came for us. As we went back upstairs, he said, "Fran's away for a few days, so I volunteered to introduce you around."

Names came at us fast—way too many to remember, although I recognized a few from bylines over stories.

"Shifts vary," Mr. Braden said. "Wire editor, layout, and electronic edition folks come in later, as does anyone covering nighttime events. This is Metro, here in the middle. Fran's desk, copyeditors, reporters."

Interrupting a tall, thirtyish man reading a *Wall Street Journal,* he said, "Harrison! Meet our summer interns, Jillian Smythe and Maggie Chen. Harrison covers local government and business."

"I do my best," Harrison said. "Where will you two be working?"

We looked at Mr. Braden.

"You'll float wherever needed. Fran's agreed to lend one of you to Photo for a while, and Sports is backlogged, so—"

"Photography!" Jillian interrupted. "I'd love that. Maggie, you don't care, do you?"

"Yes," I blurted out. "I'd much rather—"

I broke off, stopped by the way Mr. Braden was frowning, not angrily but more as if he could not believe he was going to have to deal with a couple of arguing teenagers.

Harrison's expression held a hint of amused sympathy.

"Sports will be fine," I said, which wasn't true.

"Great," Mr. Braden said. "I'll introduce you to Jake Brown. He's the editor you'll be working for this week. And then, Jillian, we'll go find the camera crew."

CHAPTER 6

It was pretty clear from the look on Jake Brown's face that I came as a surprise, though he didn't say whether it was because he'd been given extra help or because the help was me.

Whichever, there was an uncomfortable silence after Mr. Braden and Jillian left the back-corner huddle of desks that was the sports department. Jake and the other two guys there—reporters, I guessed—eyed me as though I were some sort of mystery.

"I'm Tonk," one of them said. "Welcome." Twenty-five, maybe, he had a dimpled smile that must have been really cute when he was a few years younger. He looked like he might have wrestled or played football.

"And Cody," said the other, who was about the same age and told me he wrote for online. Cody, I was guessing, had rarely seen the outdoors and never the inside of a gym.

"And that's Matilda," Cody added, pointing to a chip-nosed mannequin atop a file cabinet. Matilda wore sunglasses, a University of Washington Huskies cap, and a Washington State Cougars T-shirt. An index card pinned to her shirt asked "What's the score? Who's got the score? Does anyone know the score?"

"So," said Jake, "I suppose I need to find you work. What can you do?"

"Well . . ." There was something backward about the way this was starting out. "I wrote a regular column for my school newspaper, edited, did page design." And now I was sounding like I expected to take over the *Herald.* "I put together club notices."

"Rewrites!" Jake exclaimed. "Great! Let's get you going. You can settle at that empty desk over there—just clear the mess. Tonk will show you how the computer system works, and by then I'll have a stack of press releases for you to boil down to something short and readable."

Half an hour later I whipped out the first one: "Parents Behind Soccer will hold their first annual bake sale July 11 from nine to three-thirty on the Renton athletic field to raise funds to send their tournament-winning team to regional competition. 'The thousand-dollar goal will allow everyone to go, and not just the starters.'"

I ran it through spell check and moved it to Jake's folder, wondering why I'd been so apprehensive about beginning my job at the *Herald.*

The rewrite popped back on my screen within seconds, with the note "Ask Tonk for his style guide."

Embarrassed, I flipped through the guide until I saw I should have written "9 a.m. to 3:30 p.m.," using numerals rather than words.

The next time my rewrite came back, I changed "July 11" to "Saturday," since the bake sale would be on the Saturday immediately coming.

And the third time, there was a long note with it. "Which

Renton athletic field? What tournament? Attribution for that quote? And first annual is an oxymoron."

I was rereading the note, my face pulsing hot, when Jake said, "Maggie, stop!"

"Forget the bake sale," he said. "Give those releases to Tonk."

"I can do them," I said. "I should have known all that stuff. We have the same style guide at school, only I guess we mostly ignore it."

"Here we don't," he said.

And then, more lightly, he suggested, "Why don't you take a breather? Maybe make a fresh pot of coffee. We take turns."

"Sure," I said, not telling him that since I didn't drink coffee, I'd never actually learned to make it. I thought that making coffee couldn't be that hard. Except that one moment I was prying up the coffeepot's stuck lid, and the next moment old grounds and murky sludge were splattering everywhere. I was doing my best to clean up when Jillian went by carrying a camera bag. Beside her, a man swung along on crutches.

Tonk told me, "That's Lynch, our photo chief, after a parasailing mishap."

Jillian waved at me.

"Last year it was hang-gliding. The year before, skydiving. Each time, a broken bone. You'd think he'd get a clue he's not a bird."

Tonk was trying to make me laugh, but it didn't work. I was washing a mannequin's sunglasses, Mom's cream-colored shirt now had splotches of brown, and my boss-of-the-week was aiming compressed air at coffee grounds in his keyboard. I wanted to disappear through the floor.

Finally, after lunch, Jake found another job for me: inputting game schedules for a summer recreation section. "It would have been nice to put it out earlier," he said, "but some of the less formal leagues don't pin things down till they play their first games. Anyway, we've got enough time. You don't need to hurry. Take through Friday if you want."

"I don't work Fridays," I told him. "The intern jobs are for four days a week."

"Then through Thursday. It's just keying in data. Here's the section from last winter to show you how things should look."

Which all sounded good, except the work wasn't just inputting. It was deciphering bad handwriting on information sheets sent in by coaches and players who didn't, any two of them, have the same ideas about what to include.

It was trying to figure out which teams belonged to what leagues. The material didn't always say. Sometimes it didn't even say what the sport was.

I considered asking Tonk what some made-up abbreviations meant, but each time I looked over, he appeared so intent on his own work that I didn't.

And after the rewrite fiasco and the coffeepot mess, I couldn't bring myself to admit to Jake that I wasn't up to this job, either.

Instead of getting help, I spent the afternoon starting schedule after schedule, quitting each time I got stuck, and looking for an easier one to do. My stomach hurt, the newsroom felt as if it were about a hundred degrees, and when five o'clock came, I was so, so ready to leave.

Mom, who taught on Monday nights, had left me money for pizza. I ordered it and then switched on my computer to read what Bett and Aimee had to say.

Their joint message began with a rambling account of some very cool guys they'd met, who were in a vacation rental on the beach where my friends' families had summer cabins.

I hit the Reply button and wrote, "If there's an extra (generally perfect) boy, you might UPS him to me." I pictured them laughing, since my pickiness in boyfriend requirements was a running joke.

And then I went on to answer their questions.

"How's the *Herald*?"

I typed "Awful," deleted that, and wrote "Big." Which wasn't exactly what I meant, but it was as close as I wanted to get to saying I felt in over my head.

"Are there other interns?"

"One."

"Do you like them?"

"No."

I ate my pizza while trying to read a mystery I couldn't focus on. My thoughts kept skittering back to the disaster of the day.

And when they weren't there, they went to the real mystery in my own life.

If I was serious about trying to discover Dad's and my unknown family, I needed to call that Mr. Ames back. With Mom gone, this would be a good time to do it. But then I glanced at my watch—7:30 p.m., after ten on the East Coast. Too late to call someone I'd never met to ask questions I hadn't yet thought out.

I just hoped that when I did call, he would have some solid information to give me. And maybe he'd tell me some personal stories about Dad as well. There was so much about my father's life that I had never even wondered about.

I tossed Pepper a slice of pepperoni.

Perhaps Mr. Ames and my dad had hung around together, had fun, maybe done silly stuff. Or perhaps, working so hard, Dad didn't have time.

I suddenly remembered a picture of Dad looking ridiculous in a knobby, wire-laced helmet. He'd put it on to get a better grasp of the story he was writing about an electronic game company's new products, and someone had snapped the photo and given it to him. Mom and I had threatened to have it framed.

I asked him if the helmet had been fun to try out, and he answered that it had been both fun and uncomfortable, which he'd expected. But he'd been surprised by the overwhelming, disorienting sensation it gave of stepping into a different world.

"Research above and beyond, that I wouldn't want to repeat," he said. "And I enjoyed every minute of it!"

Then he added that if he hadn't tried out the helmet, he'd

have written his story without really understanding what he was writing about.

I wondered if we still had that photo. Had it been in Dad's office? We'd sorted through so much.

I'd sorted through so much. Letters, pictures, newspaper clippings, notebooks, drafts of articles . . .

There'd been no point in keeping the drafts, and I'd thrown most of them away, though it had seemed wrong somehow. He'd put such effort into his work. Such painstaking care, as though no comma was too small to worry over and no question too unimportant to ask. No oxymoron too insignificant to weed out.

CHAPTER 7

I arrived at the *Herald* a little early the next morning, found the file room, and got a copy of the recreation guide from the previous summer. And before starting on the inputting again, I went online and printed out the Wikipedia entries for every kind of team game played around Seattle in July and August.

It must have been ten o'clock or so when Jake stopped by my desk. I was so wrapped up in the schedule I was entering that his "How's it going?" startled me.

"Fine," I answered automatically.

Then I told him the truth. "Actually, really slowly. But I'm catching on, I think."

"Let one of us know when you want something checked." He picked up the summer guide, glanced at the field hockey page I had it turned to, and set it back down. "I should have given you this one."

When noon came, I took my lunch to the *Herald*'s employee break room and settled at the empty end of a long table, the way I had the day before, when I'd eaten by myself.

This time, though, I'd barely unwrapped my tuna sandwich when Jillian dropped into the chair opposite.

"Whoa!" she said. "Can you believe the work? Yesterday Lynch dragged me all over town carrying his camera gear, and today, do you think we're taking it easy just because he doesn't have a shoot till this afternoon? No! I spent the morning chained to a computer, looking through ten million photos of early Seattle. And why? To find one showing somebody planting a seedling tree at the arboretum decades ago—just so we can include it in a spread about how great the place is today. I told him a tree is a tree, and people know how they start."

She snapped off the lid of a plastic container, looked with distaste at the cold macaroni inside, and helped herself to the peanuts I'd brought.

"With Lynch it's just job after job," she said. "You knew what you were doing, asking to go to Sports."

"That's not how it was," I told her.

"Really?" she said, but at least she looked embarrassed. "Well, maybe not. But it's worked out, right? I mean, I don't know one thing about sports, so I'd have made a fool of myself over there, while anybody can tell, just looking at you, there's nothing you're not super-competent at."

For a moment all I could do was stare at her. And then, just in case that was truly what she thought, I said, "For your information, I did not do one thing correctly yesterday. In fact, yesterday was flat-out terrible."

"Really?" she said again, this time sounding slightly contrite. But then, brightening, she added, "But you're doing better today, right?"

"That's not the point." I took back the peanuts. "You didn't know anything about me yesterday, so you just assumed what you wanted to assume. And I let you. But I won't again."

Jillian's face got red, and I braced myself for an angry reply.

Instead she said, "Maggie, can we start over? I want us to be friends. And I'm sorry about yesterday—about the sports thing and also about being so nosy. It's none of my business if your folks are divorced or your dad's split or—"

I cut her off before her apology got any worse. "My father's dead," I said. "He was killed by a driver who didn't even stop."

Jillian's hands flew to her mouth. "Oh, Maggie, that's awful. But God will get him. The driver, I mean. Well, maybe your dad, too, if you believe in heaven. When? How did it happen?"

"In May," I answered. I again tried to stop her, not wishing to find out what she might say if she got on a real roll. "He was a journalist. He'd been away on assignment, and he got hit when he stopped on his way home from the airport."

"Oh!" she said again. "Really recent! You're still in mourning! I can imagine how hard it must be. And he was a journalist? Everything here must make you think about him."

I wanted to hug the photographer who came to tell Jillian that Lynch needed her, though I seriously doubted the message.

"Anyway," she said, "I'm glad we got things fixed between us." She reached for two of the last three peanuts. "You know, sugared pecans don't cost that much more, and they taste a lot better."

And then she rushed off in a whirl of bright clothes, leaving me to sweep up shells and think about what she'd said.

Mourning was such an odd, old-fashioned word. It brought to my mind images of black clothes and stoic dignity and of the kind of rooms with closed draperies that, in a movie, tell you right away someone has died. *Death's a fact,* such things say. *Don't question it.*

Only I had.

I'd gotten through the early days after Dad died by not totally accepting that he had. Instead I'd slipped into a want-to-believe kind of hope, like when a kid who knows that Santa doesn't exist still hopes a swoosh of winter wind might be a flying sleigh.

Except that my hope had been much bigger: a huge, aching invention that the report of Dad's death was wrong. That it was someone else who had been run over, and that the next time the phone rang, it would be Dad calling. He'd say he'd been in a remote area with no wireless connection, out of cell range, his rental car broken down.

I'd known it was all fantasy, but it had helped me more than Mom's blaming herself had helped her, which is what she'd done those first days. Made up *If onlys* with her at the center.

"If only I'd gone with him," she'd say. "If only I'd taken him to the airport and then picked him up."

One morning she'd burst out, "What was he doing there anyway, on foot, in some neighborhood he didn't know? He should have called me! I could have read him a map."

And on another day she'd slammed a table so hard that a crystal vase fell and shattered. "It's not fair! So not fair!"

And it wasn't, I thought. Not the hidden past. Not his death. Not after.

Before leaving the *Herald* parking lot that evening, I sat in the car and called Bill Ames on my cell phone. He didn't answer, and I hung up without leaving a message. And with Mom home, I didn't get a chance to try him again.

He didn't answer on Wednesday, either, when I tried calling right after work. But Mom went to the copy shop after we finished a fast dinner, and as soon as she drove away, I called once more.

"I didn't expect to hear from you again," he said once he'd placed who I was. "I had the impression you weren't too happy with what I had to say the last time."

"It surprised me," I said. "I didn't know as much about my dad as I'd thought."

He laughed. "Don't feel bad. My kids go to sleep when I tell tales from ancient history. But what can I help you with?"

"I was wondering if you ever went home with Dad, like over a holiday?"

"To California? I didn't have airfare for that. And he pretty much stayed around New York, anyway."

California? I'd never heard Dad mention living in California. But maybe it made sense. If he was considering starting his life over with a new identity, he'd have wanted to get as far away from the original one as possible. And going all the way from one coast to the other for college . . .

"Maggie? You still there?"

"Yes. Sorry. I was just thinking. Do you know where in California he lived?"

Now Mr. Ames was the one silent for a bit. Then, "If he ever mentioned it, I've long since forgotten. But I'm pretty sure it was a city rather than a rural area. Your dad had"—he paused as though considering—"he was street-smart. Manhattan didn't throw him, not even when we were freshmen."

"So you knew him all the way through college," I said. "I was wondering if you could tell me more about—"

Mr. Ames interrupted me. "Maggie, I'm facing an early morning. A trip to take, and I'm not packed. So unless there's something specific?"

"No, I guess not. Thank you," I said, and hung up.

It fit. That note of Dad's I'd seen and torn up, about a family search. There'd been something about California in that, hadn't there?

But California? Just the biggest state in the nation, population-wise. Probably with more places that qualified as cities than most states had towns.

I sat back and closed my eyes. How would I even know where to start looking for Dad's family—half of *my* family—in a place like that?

At the *Herald* on Thursday, I continued with the work that was becoming easier the better I got at deciphering disc golf and slow-pitch ball schedules. As I had the day before, I called people for information they'd forgotten to include. I verified park names and addresses in the phone book. I checked the style guide for everything, absolutely *everything* I had the least question about.

Sometimes I was tempted to take shortcuts—to tell myself a team's members would know whether a nine o'clock Saturday game was an early one or under the lights at night. But then I'd picture Dad's worked-over drafts, with leads rewritten till there could be no misunderstanding what he meant. And then I'd find out what I needed to know.

Jake or Tonk checked on my progress occasionally. They always found things for me to fix, but they found fewer each time.

And I'd learned when I could ask for help without causing them problems, because I'd gotten a better feel for the tempo of the newsroom.

I enjoyed the morning's slow start, just as I looked forward to the pace picking up in the early afternoon, the way Mr. Braden had said it would. By late afternoon the air would almost snap with the tension of stories coming together, headlines being written, pages getting finished.

The first page proofs would come off printers, and I would read a piece of the next day's paper that nobody outside the newsroom had ever seen.

When I returned to my desk after lunch, I typed one last swim meet program and then told Jake I'd finished inputting all the schedules he'd given me.

"Nice work," he said. "We're going to be sorry to lose you Monday."

"I'll miss being here," I said. "Though," I quickly added before he got any ideas, "I'm looking forward to doing something that's more hard news." I glanced at the piles of paper on his desk. "What would you like me to do next? I could try another rewrite."

"You could," he said, "but I've got a better idea. Grab your things."

"Where are we going?"

"Safeco Field. I've got an interview with a couple of the players, and I'm taking you with me. Before you leave Sports, I want you to see more than the drudge stuff."

"But a Mariners interview?" I exclaimed. "Just like that? What do I do?"

"Watch, listen, and have fun!"

Which is exactly what I did once I got done pinching myself that I was actually inside the working part of a major-league stadium, sitting across from two of baseball's superstars.

And I learned several things about interviewing. When Jake got one question answered, he didn't just jump right into the next. Instead he waited, and sometimes the wait prompted a longer answer that was a lot more interesting than the first, short one.

I've got to tell Dad, I thought once, briefly, before I remembered that I couldn't.

But then I realized Dad must have known, anyway, about listening past the time when it was tempting to talk. Maybe that's one of the things he'd have taught me if he hadn't died.

When I thanked Jake back at the *Herald,* I knew he assumed it was for taking me on the interview.

It was, partly, but it was also for having given me a job that week that I'd been able to learn from and finish.

And it was for those moments, watching Jake work, when I'd remembered the side of Dad that I knew to be true.

FAI-YI LI, 1932

Outside, Sucheng is waiting. Noisy vehicles clog streets, ship workers shout, and the chains of huge cranes clang loudly. People in strange clothing, with faces that tell me they will not know our language, hurry by carrying parcels, pulling children, pushing carts, loading trucks.

Sucheng says, "This is not what I expected."

"No," I say as a man bumps my arm and a woman with an expression of dislike steps wide around us.

Confused, I realize I should have looked to this moment. But always, since that night Sucheng and I fled, there was a closer one to be worried about. "Perhaps," I say uncertainly, "we should find Li Dewei. Perhaps he will tell us what to do."

Sucheng and I start to walk away from the docks, and when I see persons not hurrying who look kind, I show them Li Dewei's name and say one of the few American words I know, Please. *Soon I learn another word.* Chinatown.

Sucheng and I go in the direction they point, and eventually, weaving through the new smells of salt air, automobiles, grit, and green forests, I recognize the old cooking smells of charcoal and hot fat.

I see a sign with characters I can read, and then more such signs lining a street where the men look like those I grew up with.

It makes me breathe deeply with relief, though I notice that Sucheng is looking behind us, to the ways we have not taken.

I find Li Dewei when I spot his name on the sign for a hand laundry. Pulling Sucheng into the small shop with me, I tell him I am Wu Fai-yi.

He shrugs. "That means nothing."

I explain that Sucheng and I are the ones he said could be his children.

"On paper only. Why are you here?" he asks.

But his face is not as hard as his words, and he says, "Have you no plans? What did you think to do?"

Because I cannot say I did not think, *I answer, "Find work."*

"Well . . ."

My gaze follows his as he looks vaguely about, as though to find a solution to Sucheng and me in washtubs and drying clothes and stacks of flat brown paper bundles with string around them.

Outside there is a commotion. Three boys run through the crowd, knocking people aside, and angry words follow. The boys separate, one fleeing up an alley and the others disappearing into buildings as a car with markings jerks to a stop. Two men wearing uniforms get out, adding their voices to the noise, and people point this way and that. And then one of the men is entering here, and we in the laundry are no longer just watchers.

The official speaks to me in an accusing rush of words, and I understand that he mistakes me for one of the running boys.

I want to tell him that if I am red-faced and breathing fast, it is from the laundry's heat and my fright.

His hand is outstretched. "Papers," I hear, a word I know, and the only paper I have is the one given to me by the men who took my money.

Behind the official, Li Dewei looks as though to stop me from showing it, but I already have it out, and the man snatches it from me.

And then he demands something of Li Dewei, who, face graying, brings other papers that the man also reads. The man gestures at Sucheng and asks a question. I catch another word I know. "Daughter?"

And Li Dewei, after a moment, nods.

* * *

Li Dewei and I sit up late in the back room of the laundry, talking over what has happened, and Sucheng's face has an impatient set to it as she prowls the tiny space.

I think that perhaps she does not understand what Li Dewei is explaining. Who the running boys were is unimportant. What matters is that the policeman saw my identity paper with the name Fai-yi Li on it and with Li Dewei as my father.

"It is an easy thing for them to find a reason to make a person be deported," he says. "I should have remembered that when the man from a Gold Mountain firm came here with an offer of money . . ." His voice trails off as he adds, "I wanted it for my own son and wife, to finally bring them here."

"How long have you waited?" I ask.

"For my wife? Since the year before you were born. That is when I traveled to China to find a wife who would join me here. But before I had saved enough for her passage, the immigration laws changed, making it impossible. Then two years ago they changed back and I returned to make the arrangements. But the costs were much more than I had foreseen, and so I was back here, alone again, when the man came with his offer."

"So you have a real child about my age?" I ask. "I am fifteen."

He smiles. "No! A baby boy, born after my second visit."

Then Li Dewei asks me why we wanted to come to America and how we came by the money we paid the Gold Mountain firm. I tell him the first story that comes to my mind—that Sucheng and I are here because our parents arranged to send us.

All this talk buys time. Under it, he is thinking and I am thinking what to do next.

Finally he says, "The police may come back, and they will expect to find you here. I think you should stay. You can work in the laundry."

Sucheng, who is still pacing, whirls to face us. "No! I did not come here for that."

"Thank you," I tell Li Dewei. "We will do as you say."

‹ ‹ ‹

The next weeks are hard, hard, as Sucheng and I struggle to learn the work of the laundry. And I work, too, to learn the ways and words of this new country that I must get along in.

Mostly I bend over a tub of hot suds, rubbing shirts up and down over the metal ridges of a washboard. An apple hangs on a string where I can reach for a bite without moving from my work.

I stop my scrubbing only when a customer comes into the shop, and then only if Li Dewei is away or in his room upstairs. I give the customer his clothes, which are marked with his name in Chinese characters, and on a slip of paper I draw a circle to show the size of the coin he must pay. I listen to see if he murmurs the name of it.

Sucheng, ironing in the back room where all our living is done, has fewer chances to learn and more time for discontent to grow. She has no door through which to look out onto the street and no customers to learn from, and I do not know what she does with her mind.

Dream, I think. I think she still believes there is gold for the picking up, somewhere. Just not in Chinatown. Not in Seattle.

Or perhaps she remembers China, though if she does, I wonder what part she dwells on. Does she think about playing at our mother's feet, or about how hard our mother worked? Does she remember how we believed ourselves special, being twins with no brothers or sisters in a village where most children had many? Or perhaps she reflects on how imperceptibly understanding seeped into our bones that being only *also meant being* eldest: *eldest son, eldest daughter.*

Sometimes, when I take her a pile of freshly dried clothes, I see her gaze leave the hot, heavy iron she moves over a white cotton shirt. She looks frantically from wall to wall, and I wonder if she is seeking a way out of the laundry or a way back to who we were.

"It will not always be like this," I say, hoping to comfort her. "When

the authorities have forgotten Li Dewei, we can look for something better, and then—"

She does not want to wait. "Li Dewei's danger is not our problem. He took our money knowing the risk." She says, "You should not have brought me here. I would be better off home with our parents."

That is the heart of her arguments, so unfair that I must fight back resentment. I was not the one who needed to leave.

But she is also right. She could not have gotten here alone.

And so guilt runs through me because her life has become so small and because the wrongs we did weigh heavily. I worry about the time when our parents will get old without a son or daughter to care for them, and I wonder what has become of the children of that man whose body we hid. It was not their fault he attacked Sucheng.

If there were a way to go back to that moment when blood seeped into earth, a way I could make my decision over again, I think I would not give in to my sister. Instead I would insist we go to the authorities and say, This is who we are, and this is what has happened. *If need be, perhaps I would even say that I was the one who fought with the man. I would do that for Sucheng.*

She tries once more. "We can go to another city where no one has ever heard of Fai-yi Li," she says. She looks at me coyly, the way she would look at someone from whom she wanted something when she was a pretty child. Now it is grotesque. "You can go back to being Wu Fai-yi."

"No," I answer. "Not now. We will not add more harm to what we have already done. Perhaps, when Li Dewei's family is here, he will want us to leave, but until he does—"

I stop. Telling her Not now *has made a blade of fear—*What if never?*—twist like a knife in my stomach. What kind of eldest son does not carry on his family's name?*

CHAPTER 8

I jerked awake the next morning to a room full of sunlight. I bolted half out of bed, groping for my alarm clock that hadn't rung, wondering how late I was going to be getting to the *Herald.* Then I realized it was Friday, my day off.

In the kitchen I found a to-do list from Mom, but it was really chores for both of us—groceries, lawn mowing, window washing, a run to the store for cleaning supplies.

"None of this has to get done today, though," she wrote. "If you've got something better to do, go for it, and we'll cram the work into the weekend."

I wasn't sure about *better,* but I did need to go shopping, and after a quick call for permission to use her charge card against my first paycheck, I drove to the mall.

And then I spent the next few hours buying enough things so I could stop raiding her closet for work clothes.

It would have been fun if I'd known exactly what I was looking for. Still something between high school and career. Between kid and not kid. Between—

My problem was that I didn't know exactly what *between* I meant. I just wanted to look less ambiguous—more defined—than the girl in the dressing-room mirror.

Not a concept you should share with a sales clerk unless you want her to start throwing strangely cut tops and fringed belts at you.

Finally I settled on a couple of short-sleeved shirts, a pair of pants that I hoped wouldn't wrinkle as badly as my linen ones, and a tan skirt that I thought would go with anything.

And then I texted Bett and Aimee that having a job was expensive.

They texted back that they were living in their swimsuits.

At home I shook out my new clothes and ironed the pieces that needed ironing.

I did my laundry, careful first to check that the washing machine hoses and drains were functioning properly.

I mowed the yard and wondered if Mom and I could afford to hire a lawn service. Mowing was something Dad had always done, one of many things we'd counted on him for. We'd counted on him for so much.

I still couldn't get my mind around how we'd known him so well but also hadn't known him at all. Taken him for granted, I suppose.

And I still hadn't come up with any good ideas for learning where in all California he might have come from. I'd searched an online database of birth records without finding one that I thought might be his, and I hadn't figured out what to try next.

On Monday I started working on Metro, for its editor, Fran Paglioni. Most of the morning I answered the phones and helped her go through the mail, learning as I did which reporters covered what beats. I had to switch desks a couple of times in the process, for as an intern I didn't have a nest of my own. Instead I worked at whatever nearby desk was available, until the owner appeared and booted me away.

Then, after lunch, just when I was wondering where everyone had disappeared to, Fran stood up and said, "It's time for the who's-got-what session. Come on."

As we walked to a small conference room that opened off one side of the newsroom, she explained, "These sessions prep me for the daily news budget meeting that Sam Braden runs. And they give us a chance to make connections that otherwise might get missed."

I slid into a chair beside Jillian. Lynch sat on the other side of her, his crutches between them.

"Hey," Jillian whispered. "So you're here now? Maybe we can really get to know each other."

She broke off as Fran got the meeting rolling. "I think you've all met Maggie Chen by now, our other intern." She turned to the reporter on her left, a woman whose beat was the environment. "Want to start, Chris?"

"The bad water at that new medical clinic has been traced to a bankrupt machine shop. Cleanup's likely to be expensive, and the arguing about who'll foot the bill has already begun."

"Rough on everybody involved," Fran said. She made a note. "Anything else?"

"The Forest Service would like a reminder put in about campfire regulations. No hurry running it."

The education reporter promised a piece on a new prekindergarten program. Fran said it would run, but she wanted to hold another on school assignments for a day when the news hole was bigger.

I listened, fascinated by the seemingly casual way the content of the next day's newspaper got decided.

Then the man assigned to covering the courts launched into a complicated explanation of a suit involving a restaurant's method of computing hourly wages, which seemed to come down to stiffing the wait staff.

Eyes glazed over, and Fran finally interrupted. "Okay. Write it up. And if you've got any humanizing quotes, *please* throw them in."

She turned to the police reporter, Gary Maitlen. "What are you working on?"

"Got an ID on that drive-by shooting at the end of May."

Fran raised her eyebrows. "Just now? I'd forgotten about it."

"Me, too," he said, hands signaling *Sorry.* "The police withheld it pending notification of next of kin, and then . . . Anyway, you want something for tomorrow?"

"They're still treating it as a random killing?"

"Yeah, but I can lead with the angle that the investigation has gone inactive."

Someone muttered, "Talk about non-news."

Fran said, "There's nothing special about the victim?"

"Nada." Glancing at a pocket-size notebook much like those my dad had used, Gary said, "Name was Donald Landin, a mid-level city employee in one of the Eastside towns. Got killed right outside the apartment house where he lived."

"Give me a paragraph or two, but keep it short," Fran told him.

Moving on to Lynch, she asked what Photography had to offer.

Harrison, the reporter Jillian and I had met on our first day, interrupted. “Wait a sec. Maitlen, exactly when did that shooting occur?”

Gary consulted his notes again. “Friday, May twenty-third.”

I gave an involuntary start, and Fran asked, “Maggie, do you have something to add?”

I shook my head. “The date just reminded me of something personal,” I answered, without explaining that it was when Dad died coming home from the airport.

Fran’s attention switched back to Harrison, who was thumbing through his notebook.

“I thought so!” he said. “That was the day I had an appointment to meet someone who claimed to know about illegalities where he worked. When nobody showed, I figured the call was a prank.”

“And . . . ?”

“The name the caller gave was Dan Lind, which is pretty close to Donald Landin. And he specifically mentioned the Eastside. Maybe they’re the same person, and he really did know something but got caught up in the street thing before he could tell me about it.”

Fran looked dubious. “I think you’re reaching.”

“But I might not be,” Harrison argued. “I could make a quick visit to where this Donald Landin worked. Nose around some. I’ve got time this afternoon.”

Fran tapped her pencil. “All right. I guess it can’t hurt.”

"Mind if I take along one of the interns?"

Fran looked surprised, but then her puzzlement cleared. "Cover? Okay by me. You game, Maggie?"

"Sure," I said quickly, hardly believing my good fortune. Was I actually being sent out on a real—or possibly real—story?

Jillian leaned forward, and I braced myself. If she tried to grab this assignment, I was going to grab back.

But she didn't say anything, and Fran, with a nod, moved on.

CHAPTER 9

"So," I said to Harrison as we drove out of the parking lot, "what did Fran mean about *cover?*"

"You'll see," he said, turning on music full blast and heading for the Evergreen Point Floating Bridge across Lake Washington, out of Seattle and to the towns to the east. Then, relenting, he turned the music off. "You're going to be my excuse to look around," he said.

"What do you want me to do?"

"Appear eager. And keep your eyes and ears open. We might not find a story, but fishing expeditions are part of the job. The most interesting part, sometimes."

"I know," I said. "That's what my dad—"

He prompted, "Your dad?"

"He was a reporter," I said. "And I was just remembering how he used to say pretty much the same thing. That part of what keeps a newsman going are the possibilities."

Harrison chuckled. "I've never heard it put that way, but it's true. Only you said *was.* What's he doing now?"

"He died recently. But before that, he covered business news for—"

Harrison interrupted. "Maggie *Chen!* Of course! Steven Chen was your father? I've read enough of his work to know how good he was."

He was silent a moment and then said rather awkwardly, "I

read about the accident. I'm sorry. I guess he'd have been pretty proud of you doing this internship."

"I don't think he'd have been all that proud last week," I said. "Not at the beginning, anyway. I got off to a pretty rocky start."

Harrison grinned. "My first morning in a newsroom—this was back in the day—I erased an editor's hard drive. Did you do anything that egregious?"

"I got coffee grounds on the Sports mannequin."

"Not even in the same league."

The city hall where Donald Landin had worked was a new-looking, well-landscaped building. Before leaving the *Herald,* Harrison had gotten Gary Maitlen to find out exactly what department Landin had worked in, and now, scanning a lobby directory, I said, "Planning and Development is on the second floor. Do we just go up?"

"Let's first see what's on people's minds," Harrison said, heading for a bulletin board a little way down a wide corridor.

The board held public notices—an opening on the city council, changes in the leash law—and memos to employees. Someone wanted to start a lunchtime walking program. Volunteers were sought to organize a family picnic.

A woman in the office opposite called, "May I help you?"

Harrison introduced us both and then said, "Maggie's a high school intern with the *Herald.* She wants to learn what journalism is all about, so I thought I'd show her the inside of a city hall. This looks like a pleasant place to work."

"It is," the woman said. "Everybody gets along. Not that there aren't stresses." She pointed to a PAY TRAFFIC FINES HERE sign on the next desk. "Customers can be difficult."

"I can imagine," Harrison said, laughing. "But good co-workers—that goes a long way. How about the elected officials? Are they a good group?"

"Pretty much," she said. "Though I don't have contact with them the way people in some of the other departments do." She picked up a pen. "You two are welcome in any of the public offices. You want directions, just ask someone."

Harrison took me into each office along the first-floor hall—Animal Control, Streets, Parks and Recreation—and in each one he gave the same speech about showing the *Herald*'s intern the inside of a city hall.

I noticed that he timed our entrances to coincide with moments when all the clerks in an office were either on the phone or dealing with other people. Which gave us time to study more bulletin boards, as well as to read any papers left lying about.

"So, did you get anything from all that?" I asked when we finally reached the staircase.

"A feel for who's who," he said, "and for how things are going. If I had to make a guess, I'd say the mayor is in over his head trying to run a town that's growing faster than anyone expected it to."

"You must have read something that I didn't," I said.

"No. I'm just making inferences from things like his proposal for a moratorium on new building permits pending a catch-up on the applications already in process."

The reception we got in the Planning and Development office backed up Harrison's assessment. The harried employee that Harrison approached told him, "There's nothing here for your intern to see. And if there were, there'd be nobody with time to show it to her."

Blowing right by the dismissal, Harrison said, "I heard one of your people got killed in a street shooting not long ago. Must be hard to lose someone that way. And, of course, there'd have been all his work to deal with."

"Landin had already quit," the man said. "But you're right about his work being a problem. He hadn't been replaced—still hasn't—and the rest of us are way too overloaded to take on his stuff."

"Tell me about it," Harrison said, all sympathy.

"It's only getting worse," the man went on. "The city council's planning committee has to approve any recommendations we make, and it's not moving on anything and won't before next week." He suddenly frowned. "You're not writing this up, are you?" he asked. "Because if you are, that was all off the record."

Harrison nodded. "Understood. But what's brought the planning committee to a standstill?"

"Missing a person and nobody in charge. Toby Yeager, the city councilman who ran it for years, died of a stroke a couple of months ago."

"And what happens next week?"

"The council, when it meets, will finally get around to appointing someone to finish out his term and, I hope, get some movement going here. Look, I really do have to get back to work."

Before leaving the building, Harrison and I stopped by the

mayor's office to ask for a list of people who'd applied for the council position.

The person we spoke to said, "We're still verifying their qualifications. All the names will be on the city's website when it's updated tomorrow."

Fran was looking over page proofs when we got back to the newsroom. Seeing us, she asked, "Find out anything?"

"Nothing specific," Harrison answered. "But things are unsettled enough out there that I'd like to do a little more checking around."

Fran asked me, "And how'd you do?"

"Great!" I said. "I listened, and I learned that you don't always ask outright what you want to know."

"Nope. Not when you don't know what you're looking for. Or when you're looking for something folks might want to hide." She turned back to Harrison. "So . . . ?"

"Give me one more day. And if Maggie wants to keep helping, that would be great."

"Sure," I said. "More cover?"

"No way," Harrison answered. "Tomorrow we roll up our sleeves and get to work." He raised his eyebrows as though asking if I'd really meant that *sure.* "It'll be toiling at the computer. Not nearly as much fun as slinging around coffee grounds."

"That was not fun," I said. "And today was. Today—"

I broke off, knowing I'd feel ridiculous telling him I felt as if my world had opened wider. But I did.

Sure I'd been in government buildings before, usually with Mom, but this time I hadn't been a bystander. This time I'd had a job to do, even if it was only to provide Harrison with an excuse so he could do his. And that had kept the city hall from being just another building filled with people I didn't notice. It had made it a particular, individual piece of the world, and for a short time I'd been part of it.

Finally I just said, "Today was more what I hoped for."

FAI-YI LI, 1933

Li Dewei comes and goes, making arrangements to bring his wife and son over, and he grows more excited as the time for their sailing draws near.

And indeed, it does seem that he will be ready for us to be gone. They will need the space Sucheng and I take up, and since the policemen have not returned, the danger that they will come back threatens less and less.

Meanwhile, my learning continues, so that this time when we go out on our own, I will be prepared.

At night, when I am free to leave the laundry, I go to where chop suey restaurants—such American food!—bring people from other parts of the city. They wear bright clothes and talk and laugh loudly and walk as though they have a right to more space than their bodies have need for. They do not notice me step into the street to make way.

They do not see me listening, either—following sometimes, to hear them talk. For I need to learn not just the words of my new language but also the sounds, which are difficult to form and must be spoken in unfamiliar rhythms.

During the day, I practice the sounds and patterns in my head. And because my speaking is improving, when a customer comes in, I try out the new things I know. "Two dimes," I say, without drawing any picture.

Li Dewei, on his way out one afternoon, stops to watch and listen. The customer gives me a quarter, which I know, too, and I give him a five-cent piece back.

When the customer leaves, Li Dewei hands me paper money. "Do you know how much this is?" he asks.

"One dollar."

"Do you know how many dimes make one dollar?"

"Ten."

"Then take this dollar to the herbalist whose shop is on the corner two blocks over. Tell him it is for something to ease the ache in my knees."

I have not left my work during the daytime before, and my feet fly in the freedom of the sunshine.

' ' '

The two blocks take me to a more prosperous area, with buildings where families have private living quarters above stores much bigger than Li Dewei's laundry. I have walked through it at night but never before gone inside any place.

The herbalist's shop is fitted well, with fine cabinets of many small drawers. A call bell stands on the counter, but I hesitate to ring it in case it is for important customers only.

I hear footsteps on back stairs and then see a curtain move and a girl slip into the shop. "May I help you?" she asks.

I ask if I might see the herbalist.

"That is my father," she says. "He is away just now. But if what you want is something simple, I might be able to get it for you."

Then the door opens, and a man who appears American steps inside. Excusing herself to me, the girl gives him a small, already prepared bundle and receives payment for it. I am impressed that she talks with him in his own language, and I would ask her how she learned, except it would be rude.

So I only tell her I have come for medicine for Li Dewei, and I watch her open a ledger and run her finger down lines of handwritten words, looking, I realize, for his name. It surprises me. Reading is not a thing Sucheng or her friends at home ever learned.

"Here," the girl says. "Here is what my father gives him. I can get this for you. It will be eighty cents."

She takes the dollar and gives me back two dimes in change.

"Twenty cents," I say, so she will know that I know.

Then she pulls out one of the higher drawers and brings it to the counter along with a scale. She carefully weighs out a small quantity of dried leaves before saying, "I've never seen you before."

I explain that my sister and I have come from China only some months earlier.

"And what is your name?" she asks. So forward she is, asking, but her voice is so soft and her face so smooth I do not hold it against her.

"Fai-yi Li," I answer. "And you are called?"

"An Huang."

I have learned something about her, for she has not said Huang An, *in the way of Chinese. But then I have not said* Li Fai-yi, *either. I hope she has noticed that, also.*

"Do you always work here for your father?" I ask.

"Only sometimes, when he is very busy or away. I am still in school, and that takes most of my time."

Another surprise! A girl old enough to be married—she looks to be fourteen, perhaps fifteen—not only reading, but going to school!

She wraps the medicine in a square of paper. "I will tell my father when he returns that we now have a new customer." Then she smiles. "I hope you are happy that you have come to this country."

"Thank you," I tell her. "Yes."

I go to the door then, wondering if perhaps one day there will be need for more ache medicine, so that I might have reason to return. I glance back and see her reaching to replace the herb drawer, and then . . .

I am not sure what happens—perhaps an edge catches—but in the next instant the drawer is falling. An Huang gives a little cry as dried leaves shower down. "Oh!" she says, sounding so distressed. "Oh, no!"

So I go back in, and for many minutes we work together, picking up leaves and gently blowing to clean them. Finally we sweep up all the leaf dust too fine to save.

"Now," I tell her, looking at the quantity we have returned to the drawer, "surely this is enough that your father will not beat you."

"Not beat—" She looks astonished. "Is that what you thought? That I would be punished for dropping the drawer?"

I nod. Yes, of course, that was what I thought. It was what happened to my sister, back in China, when she was clumsy in the kitchen. It was how you taught girls to be careful.

But this An Huang says, "My father would never do that. I was only upset because I thought how hard it might be for him to replace what I had spilled. Sometimes American officials make getting Chinese medicines very difficult." Then she smiles again. "Thank you for helping me. Many boys might have run off rather than take a chance on staying and being blamed for any loss."

"I did not think of that," I tell her.

"I know," she says. "That is what I mean"—a comment that does not quite follow but makes me feel good.

I do leave then, saying goodbye in my best American.

She might answer in my language, but she does not. She gives me the respect of answering also in American, so quickly that I must repeat the sounds over and over to myself until I have puzzled them into words.

She has said, "I'll be seeing you."

· · ·

At first I suppose she meant that perhaps Li Dewei would send me to make another purchase for him, and I am impatient for him to need more herbs.

Then one fall day, when I look up from my work, I see her walking by. Other girls are with her, and she does not slow her steps. But I see the quick glance she gives the sign above the door, and her quicker glance inside.

After that, they go by on another day, and then another, until soon my days are measured against the time in the late afternoon when I might see her. She and her friends, in their school uniforms of dark blue with white collars, remind me of chattering magpies. She alone, though, looks for this place, glancing in, her eyes seeking me.

And so, again, the shape of my life changes, and I gradually cease to think of the laundry and of my new name as things for now only. Because now I am knowing An, and to her I am Fai-yi Li, Li Dewei's son, who belongs.

CHAPTER 10

Harrison and I were among the first arrivals in the newsroom on Tuesday morning.

"Where do we start?" I asked. He was setting up a laptop for himself so that I could use the computer on his desk.

"With the Department of Planning and Development postings," he answered. "I'd like to see what Landin worked on."

He showed me how to navigate the city's website. The development review area was organized by neighborhood, and there were at least ten, maybe fifteen of those. You clicked on one, and that brought up pages that showed the names and locations of individual projects, along with who had proposed them. Details included each project's review or construction status and also contact information for the Planning Department employee the project had been assigned to.

"There must be two or three dozen projects just in this first neighborhood," I said. "What are we looking for, besides Landin's name?"

"Anything unusual."

Harrison had the scroll button pressed down. "Here's Landin here, and here . . ." he said. "So it looks like that guy yesterday was right saying they haven't gotten around to reassigning Landin's work. Why don't you compile a list of everything with his name on it, and meanwhile I'm going to make some calls. I'd like to know why he quit his job."

Harrison pulled out a phone book, but I could see him watching me until I'd selected the details of the first Landin project and copied them to a blank word-processing document.

An hour later I handed him a printout.

"Spot any patterns?" he asked.

"No," I answered. "Except that, depending on the neighborhood, it's all either housing subdivisions or office buildings. How about you?"

"I learned that Landin left without giving notice or a reason—just cleared out his desk and was gone the same day."

Harrison skimmed the printout. "The big-money stuff looks like it's all being done by the same two or three construction outfits."

He gave me time to think out the next step, nodding approval when I said, "So I should go through everything again, looking for their names instead of Landin's."

"Right. I'll help this time."

The next printout made Harrison exclaim, "Bingo!"

"What?"

"Look," he said, dragging a highlighter across one item and another and then two more. The applicant on each one was Galinger Construction, and Landin was listed as the staff contact for each.

Puzzled, I said, "Yeah. I got those when I printed out Landin's list."

"Exactly!" Harrison said. "And now, with this list of all the Galinger Construction projects in front of you, do you see any *not* assigned to Landin?"

"No."

"And do you see any other big construction and development outfits whose projects are confined to just one member of the Planning Department?" Harrison didn't wait for me to check. "The answer's no to that, too."

"But how'd you spot it so fast?" I asked.

"It's what I was looking for."

He turned his monitor so I could see the display. "That's the agenda for next week's city council meeting," he said. "Read the list of applicants for the unexpired term of that councilman who died."

Third on the list was a Ralph Galinger. Clicking on the link for information about him, Harrison said, "What do you want to bet Mr. Galinger has ties to a construction company?"

He did.

Ralph Galinger, the city council candidate, was head of Galinger Construction.

"Isn't that a conflict of interest?" I asked.

"Potentially," Harrison answered, "but since he's not hiding his business, probably not. What I'd like to know is whether he's hiding some deal he had with Landin. If so, that might explain his desire to hold public office."

Harrison went back to our last printout while I tried to work out what he might be thinking.

I said, "Because if Landin was giving Galinger a pass on things—maybe getting paid to recommend approval of projects he shouldn't have—now that Landin is dead, Galinger might be afraid that whoever takes over will spot the funny stuff."

"Exactly," Harrison said. "And maybe Galinger wants on the inside of city hall so he can cover it up."

"Would Landin have that much authority?" I asked.

"I don't know," Harrison said. "Depends on how slack the oversight was."

Time disappeared as we pored over the material. We'd touched on what just might be a story—if we could find something solid to grab on to. If we could get a good enough hold to know its shape and size.

When Harrison said he was going to go eyeball the Galinger Construction projects to see if they matched the listings, I grabbed my bag.

"No," he said. "I'd rather you stay at the computer. Google around on everybody's names and on anything else you can think of. Just see what you find."

I started with Donald Landin and pretty much zeroed out.

Then I put Galinger Construction into the browser and got to a company homepage that featured Galinger's photo. He looked like he was in his forties or early fifties, fit and tanned in a golf-course kind of way. Brown hair. An open smile.

Googling on his name took me to several community projects where he'd given time or other support. It also left me slogging through links to Galingers who might or might not be the one we were interested in, such as a military reunion site that listed a Ralph Galinger among its organizers.

I thought of Tobias Yeager, the deceased city councilman and board member. Harrison had said to look at everybody.

The browser turned up Yeager's obituary and a lot of stuff related to his city council work. Again, I went into page after page that turned out to be about other people with similar names. I'd just clicked on another site when Jillian flopped down in Harrison's chair.

"Surfing?" she asked. "I wish Lynch would give me some time to play around. Isn't this about when the Nordstrom's pre-season sale happens? Or is that in August? They've probably got it online, if you just—"

"I'm not playing around, Jillian. I'm working on a story."

"Oh! Excuse me. Still that dead guy thing?" She looked at the page that was loading onto my screen. It was from a fund-raiser at a Virginia private school eight years earlier and included a picture of a family, everyone smiling. "Is that him?"

A caption popped up: "Mr. and Mrs. T. Andrew Yeager and their three children."

"No," I said, hitting the Close button.

"You know," Jillian said, "there ought to be an Internet law that old pages get wiped out."

The screen hadn't changed, so I hit Close again. Instead of taking me back to Google, it opened a bigger version of the same picture above a longer caption.

"And another requiring people who put up webpages to know what they're doing!" Jillian suggested. "So, are you and Harrison really onto something? Because that's just great if you are. I mean, I don't mind a bit that it's you instead of me. Well, maybe a little bit. But—"

Fortunately, she was interrupted by Lynch hailing her from across the newsroom. "Honestly," she said, "what now? Did I tell you he's even got me setting up shoots for him? As though he can't work a telephone on crutches. I don't know how that man got along without me."

I resumed work in what, in her wake, felt like a cocoon of quiet. And then Harrison called to ask how I was doing and to say traffic was making his job take longer than he'd expected.

"But another thing," he said. "I think there's a state site where you can look up construction companies that do business in Washington. Will you check it?"

"Sure," I said, already clearing the browser to start a new search.

I found both the site and the Galinger Construction entry pretty quickly, surprised that so much information was easy to get—business license details, address, phone, owners' names and roles, bonding, insurance . . .

Something was nagging at me, though. Some connection to something I'd seen, only I couldn't think what.

Frustrated, I pulled up the search history list and started going back through the dozens of places I'd been. It took me a while, and mostly I felt as if I were floundering.

But at least I *had* the history list, since I'd been able to stay on Harrison's computer.

Harrison didn't return until almost four o'clock.

"Find anything?" I asked.

"I'm not sure," he answered. "The Galinger projects all appear to be as billed, although I'm surprised a couple of them got city approval. One has houses going up on what sure looks like a floodplain, and another is a high-rise office building smack in the middle of a residential area." He leaned back against the desk. "I don't know if this is a wild-goose chase or not. Did you find the state site? Any complaints on file for Galinger's outfit?"

"No complaints," I told him, "and nothing more on Landin. But . . ."

I tried to deadpan it, but there was no way I could keep a grin from breaking through. "How would you like a connection between Galinger Construction and Tobias Yeager, the deceased planning committee chairman whose city council seat Galinger wants?

Harrison's reaction was all I could have asked for.

CHAPTER 11

Harrison pulled his tie loose as he took a close look at the outdated webpages I brought up. "Look at the names under the enlarged photo," I said, pointing to the caption that began "T. Andrew Yeager, Theresa Yeager . . ."

"You think T. Andrew and Tobias are the same guy?"

"I went through stories about Tobias Yeager until I found one with a good photo. They're the same person. He's just younger here. But it's the kids that are important: "children, Mary, Raul, and Luis Munez."

I handed Harrison the printout I'd made of the state listing for Galinger Construction. "Read the names of the principal owners."

Ralph Galinger
J. A. Garcia, custodian for Mary Munez
J. A. Garcia, custodian for Raul Munez
J. A. Garcia, custodian for Luis Munez

For a moment Harrison was actually speechless.

"Of course," I said, "it could be coincidence."

"Anyone who puts faith in coincidences doesn't belong in a newsroom. But it could be a legitimate business association." He humphed. "The children have a different last name, so they're probably hers from an earlier marriage."

"The Yeagers were divorced, too," I said. "His obituary didn't list any survivors, and Mrs. Yeager and the kids still live in Virginia. I tied them all to the same phone number there."

"So the question is what they're doing owning stock in Galinger Construction, which is a local company. And also, who is J. A. Garcia? Any answers there?"

"There are a bunch of Garcias in Virginia that might be him," I said, "but only one phone book listing for that name in the whole Seattle area."

"So let's call it."

An automated recording told us we'd reached a number no longer in service.

Harrison took out his notebook. "I'm going to think about what to ask and then call Theresa Yeager."

I gave him the number and then returned to a computer map program I'd opened before. I already had a few pushpins on it, marking Galinger's business and home and the address that went with the disconnected Garcia phone number. Now I entered another address into the search box. The program was still finding it when I heard Harrison place his call and identify himself. "Mrs. Yeager? This is Ed Harrison. I'm a reporter with . . ."

Harrison's side of the conversation consisted of a few questions and a lot of *I see*'s.

Finally he hung up and filled me in. "Yeager's ex-wife has never heard of Galinger Construction, and her children are most certainly not part owners of it." He looked into the distance, thinking out loud. "So now what? Start looking for Garcia, I suppose. Though how—"

"I know a starting place," I said, eyes on my computer screen. "Look here."

The map program had found the last address I'd put in, and now there was a new pushpin on the map.

"You see those two pins that are right next to each other?" I said. "The one on the right is the address that goes with that disconnected Garcia phone number. And the other is where Tobias Yeager lived."

We talked a while longer, trying to figure out how the pieces might all fit together.

Harrison said, "Let's suppose the real connection was between Galinger and Yeager, and it was not legitimate. Maybe Yeager was the one taking payoffs in return for seeing that Galinger Construction projects got approved. He could have used the kids' identities as a way for Galinger to funnel the money to him."

"Through Yeager's neighbor, Garcia."

"That's my guess. On the Galinger books it would have looked like the kids' share of any profits was being mailed to a custodian charged with handling their finances while they're minors."

"But why would Garcia take part?"

Harrison shook his head. "Don't know, but money's a good motivator. The amount involved would have to be enough to make risking jail worthwhile." He rubbed his face. "One thing, anyway. With a home in that ritzy a neighborhood, he's not going to just disappear."

He pushed back. "You ready to see Fran and then Sam Braden?"

"Mr. Braden?"

"He's responsible for what we do. He needs to know what we're working on."

"I suppose, except . . ." I paused. "Harrison, if we're right, then Yeager used his kids, or step-kids, rather. Taking their names, it was like he stole who they are. That was really, really wrong."

Harrison was watching me, waiting. "Yes?"

"I was just thinking about what he did, and how. There are so many ways to lie."

"Yep. Lots of ways. Lots of reasons. Many shades of truth. Let's go."

We had a quick talk with Fran, and then we all headed for Mr. Braden's office, a large, glass-enclosed space on one side of the newsroom.

Harrison ran through all we'd done and then recapped our speculations. "We think that Tobias Yeager, on the city council and chairing the planning committee, might have made sure some iffy Galinger Construction projects got through. In return, Ralph Galinger would have kicked back payments to Yeager by disguising them as profits being distributed to people with an ownership interest in Galinger Construction, three of whom were Yeager's ex-step-kids. Except that the kids and their mother never saw or even knew about the money, because it went to a supposed custodian who handed it over to Yeager, probably in return for a share."

"Those are some pretty major guesses," Mr. Braden said. "And ugly, if they're right."

Fran said, "I hate untangling white-collar crime. Give me a straight-out murder any day!" Then she closed her eyes a moment, murmured, "I didn't mean that," and said to Harrison, "You got into this because of Donald Landin. How does he fit in?"

"My guess is that Yeager was paying him to make sure the planning office didn't red-flag any of the Galinger projects. Maybe Landin got scared and saw whistle-blowing as a way out, and that's when he called me, fudging his name."

Mr. Braden studied the *Herald* logo on his coffee mug. "It would be nice to get into the company books and see where any profit distributions were actually mailed, but that's not going to happen. I want every state record verified, though. And Galinger talked to tomorrow."

We discussed the story a while longer, reviewing the material Harrison and I had accumulated. We listed alternate sources where we might double-check what we'd already found. Then Mr. Braden asked if we had anything else on Garcia.

"No," Harrison answered, "but I thought I'd scout out his address before knocking off for the day."

CHAPTER 12

"Can I go with you?" I asked Harrison, who was closing down the computers.

"It's too near quitting time," he answered. "I won't be coming back."

"I can drive my own car and then go home from there."

When I got a nod, I grabbed my bag and started for the side door.

"Hey!" he said. "Where are you going?"

"Around to the parking lot."

"No one's shown you the shortcut?"

He led me down a back stairway and through solid doors into an echoing concrete space that smelled of news ink. A beeping forklift backed up with a huge roll of paper. Two men punched switches at a lighted control panel. And beyond them . . .

Beyond them, on the other side of a long expanse of glass, the *Herald*'s massive presses ran, all spin and speed and *whirr* and *clack* and endless, flowing ribbons of paper.

"Oh!" I said, stopping, enthralled. *"Oh!"*

Harrison, bending to be heard over the racket, said, "I never get tired of watching."

“I can see why,” I said. “But why are the presses going now? The paper won’t be ready until tonight.”

“Probably printing one of the Sunday sections that get done days ahead.” From a pile of discarded pages, some with blurred type, some too light to be legible, Harrison picked up one of the better ones. “Looks like the monthly business roundup,” he said.

I nodded, recognizing it. Dad’s news agency stories had sometimes run there.

Harrison must have realized what I was remembering, because he said, “Whenever I read one of your father’s pieces, I learned something I needed to know.”

“Dad used to say a story was worth writing if it made a difference to even one person.”

“He was right,” Harrison said. “You must have been pretty proud of him.”

“I was.”

The presses were moving so fast, pulling paper over rollers, pulling on my feelings.

“I was proud of my dad,” I repeated. “I guess I still am.”

Harrison’s eyebrows went up in a question.

“I’ve been thinking a lot about him lately. Wondering who he actually was.”

“I suppose kids don’t ever really know their parents,” Harrison said. “Certainly they don’t know what their parents’ lives are like outside their family.”

“I used to think I knew him,” I said.

Chunk, chunk, chunk, chunk, chunk. Blades sliced, folding metal arms flew up and down, and the streaming lines of paper became sections of the *Herald.*

I said, "Ever since we started tracking down the Galinger thing, Dad has been on my mind, sort of hovering in the back."

"Maybe because you've gotten a taste of the kind of hard digging for stories that he did," Harrison said.

We continued to watch the hypnotizing presses. "He loved this," I said. "Newspapers, I mean."

"I do, too," Harrison said. "But they're changing. They've already altered in ways few people would have imagined a decade or two ago. Fewer, smaller pages. Shifting revenue streams."

"Because people are going to the Internet and things like wireless delivery," I said, thinking about how Mom already got her magazines on an electronic book reader that fit into her purse. "But the *Herald*'s doing both, putting out a paper and an online edition."

"Yes. And nobody knows whether it will be a good partnership or one will kill the other."

I glanced at him quickly. "You don't mean that? That you think newspapers might truly go away?"

He looked serious and sad enough that I knew he did, but he answered, "Not really. I hope not. Hard copy serves functions that cyberspace just can't, not the least of which is giving readers the pleasure of holding a physical newspaper. Though," he added, "that can be a mixed pleasure." Grinning, he showed me his hands, which were smudged from the over-inked, discarded page he'd picked up.

I laughed with him, but the conversation left me uneasy. It added, actually, to a different uneasiness that had been increasingly nagging at me ever since I'd thought how the Munez kids were possibly being hurt. As we started walking again, I asked, "Harrison, what if we're wrong?"

"About?"

"About this story we're working on. What if we're so focused on digging up a crime that we're putting together a picture that's not real? That's just going to make trouble for people who haven't actually done anything wrong."

"If we don't find wrongdoing, we won't write a story."

I nodded. I knew that. But it didn't really answer my question, because I hadn't asked exactly what I meant. I tried again.

"Say we do find that Landin, Galinger, Yeager, and Garcia all did a lot of illegal things. They'll deserve getting found out. But there'll be other people who'll get dragged into it. Their families, who might not know anything about the illegal stuff."

Harrison shook his head. "It's a good thing to keep in mind—to have an awareness of who's going to be touched by any story you write—but you can't let it stop you. Innocent people do get caught up in bad things."

His answer wasn't very satisfactory, and we didn't say any more as we made our way through a newspaper bundling area, across a loading dock, and finally to a small door that opened directly onto the employee parking lot. As Harrison opened it, I said, "What you told me about how the news business is changing. Maybe if my dad somehow could see it in a few years, he wouldn't know it anymore."

"Oh, I think he would," Harrison said. "How journalists do our jobs might change, but what we're doing won't. A country like ours—a democracy—depends on a population that knows what's going on, and people depend on us to find out and tell them."

Then, looking a little embarrassed, he said, "Enough of the civics lesson. You make me talk too much."

Still holding open the door, he, too, looked back toward the speeding, noisy, magical presses. He said, "Let's both hope those run a long, long time."

CHAPTER 13

The address the phone book gave for Garcia wasn't a proper house at all, but an abandoned-looking, made-over garage facing a side street. I said to Harrison, "That doesn't look like a place where somebody's financial custodian would live."

"Nope," he agreed. "But the house that goes with it . . ."

That house was big and looked expensive. It faced a wide tree-lined street and had a FOR SALE sign anchored in the front lawn. And we both knew who had owned it.

"So now what?" I asked.

"Well." Harrison surveyed the neighborhood.

A commercial lawn crew was finishing up a job next door. Farther along, a teenager with a basketball practiced jump shots. On the corner opposite, a woman walked a terrier.

"Excuse me," Harrison called, and went over to her. I tagged after. "We're looking for a Mr. Garcia, but . . ."

"I don't think he lives around here," the woman said. "I know all my neighbors."

Leaning down to pet her dog, Harrison said, "These days most neighborhoods aren't so close-knit that people can say that. But I suppose houses around here don't go on the market very often. Though"—he gestured toward the FOR SALE sign—"it looks like somebody's moving."

"I wish it were just a move," the woman said. "That was Toby Yeager's place. Perhaps you read about him in the paper? Poor man—a city councilman, involved in all sorts of good causes—healthy one minute and then dead of a stroke the next."

"I'm sorry to hear that," Harrison said. "I suppose the renovated garage goes with the property?"

"Handyman's quarters," the woman said, "though the handyman cleared out right after Toby died. No loyalty, and the lawn was half a foot high before the real estate agency had somebody come cut it."

"Do you know the handyman's name?" Harrison asked. "Could it have been Garcia?"

"Oh!" the woman said. "I thought you were looking for one of our regular residents. Perhaps that was his name. I wouldn't know."

Ralph Galinger was delighted when Harrison called him early Wednesday morning requesting an interview.

"About my application for the vacant city council seat?" Galinger's booming voice carried well beyond the phone. "Sure! Sure! I'll be glad to fill you in on my vision for the town."

"Actually," Harrison said, "I've got a range of things I'd like to ask you about."

"Nothing to hide. I've got to be out your way for a lunch meeting. What if I stop in at the *Herald* about eleven a.m.?"

He strode into the newsroom exactly on time.

"You want me to disappear?" I asked Harrison, hoping the answer would be no.

"Why? This is your story, too," he said, rising to shake Galinger's hand and introduce me.

"Glad to meet you, young lady," Galinger said. "Always like to see an ambitious young person."

He told Harrison, "I'm not going to stay, though. I appreciate your wanting to do a piece on me. My first thought was that it'd be good publicity, and any businessman—or potential politician—appreciates that."

He waited for Harrison to chuckle along with him.

"But on reflection," he continued, "I've decided to ask you to hold off. While I'm glad to help out my town, I don't want anyone to think I'm capitalizing on Toby Yeager's death."

"I doubt anyone would jump to wrong conclusions, whatever coverage we give," Harrison said, his voice neutral. "But it would help if you'd fill me in on a couple of things. Please, take a seat."

Galinger sat—reluctantly, I thought. His gaze skimmed the desktop, where a copy of the *Herald* was turned to the sports pages. "You a golfer?" he asked Harrison. "Because anytime you'd like a round at my country club . . ."

"I'll keep the offer in mind," Harrison said. He picked up a pencil and notepad. "So I gather you did know Mr. Yeager?"

"Certainly. We served together on a couple of nonprofit boards, helped with fundraising efforts for the hospital, that sort of thing. Not that my good works begin to come close to Toby's. Now, if you want to write about someone, a piece on him—"

"We'll consider it," Harrison said. "But getting back to you. I was wondering if you had any other ties to Mr. Yeager. Business ties, perhaps?"

"No, no." Galinger shifted in his chair. "I'm just a builder, while Toby . . ." He paused, seeming to search his memory. "Why, I don't know that I ever heard what line he was in. Suppose I always assumed he had investments, maybe family money."

Harrison nodded, then said, "I meant to ask you about Galinger Construction. Running it must be a full-time job. You don't think that would conflict with the civic duties you want to take on?"

"Oh, I don't do much hands-on work with the business anymore," Galinger said easily. "And of course, if I do get on the council, I'll step down as head of my company for the duration—wouldn't want to give even the appearance of impropriety."

"Sounds as if you've thought things out," Harrison said. "So, as chair of the city's planning committee, Yeager never gave you special help on any of your projects?"

"No!" Galinger looked indignant. "Special help because he was my friend? Of course not!" Then his expression smoothed. "But I suppose that's a newsman's question you've got to ask."

He reached across the desk, picked up the sports section, and then dropped it. "The *Herald*'s a good newspaper," he said. "That's why I still advertise in it. Shoot a lot of money your way despite people telling me I can get more value online."

"Noted," Harrison said, writing something down. Then he asked, "About your construction projects—did Yeager have a financial interest in any of them?"

This time Galinger's offended expression stayed. "Of course not. And that implication really is going too far."

"Sorry." Harrison made another note. "How about the planning office staff? Donald Landin seems to have worked on all your projects. How well did you know him?"

A pulse began to throb in Galinger's neck. "I didn't. I have my own staff to liaise with city employees. Lindan? I don't even know the name."

"Landin," Harrison corrected. "But getting back to you and Yeager. So you two didn't share business interests. How about you and any of Yeager's family?"

"Never met any of them," Galinger answered shortly. Then, seeming to regret his rudeness, he said, "Sorry. But Toby was divorced, you know."

"That's what I understand," Harrison said. "I've only a couple more questions. Maggie—"

Galinger broke in. "Look, I don't know what you're going after, but you've got my word there was never a more honest man than Toby Yeager. If you do write a piece on him, I hope you'll present him as the dedicated town leader he was. And if you must write about me, I hope you'll be fair. Remember, I didn't have to come in here."

He looked at his watch. "I'll have someone fax you my biography and a bit about Galinger Construction. And now I really must leave."

"Of course," Harrison said. "But first . . . Maggie, didn't you have a question about something you found?"

For a moment my mind went blank. Then, "Munez," I said. "Mary, Raul, and Luis Munez. We were wondering about your relationship to them."

A dark flush coursed up the sides of Galinger's face, and he leaned forward so far that Harrison must have felt his breath. "I never heard of them," he said. "And now stop wasting my time."

"You've never heard of three of Galinger Construction's principal owners?" Harrison repeated. "Interesting." He took his time writing. "I want to make sure I quote you correctly on that. And what about a J. A. Garcia?"

Galinger stood abruptly. "Who's your editor?" he demanded. "I want to see him."

"Sam Braden," Harrison answered. "I'll introduce you."

I didn't get invited to that conference, although Harrison motioned me to move to a desk close enough to the glass sides of Mr. Braden's office that I heard most of the louder parts.

The last thing Galinger said before hurrying out, anger marking every long-strided step, was, "You'll be hearing from my attorney, Braden, if you print one word."

"What are we going to do?" I asked after I'd been waved in to take the chair still warm from Galinger.

"Write it up," Fran answered. "Galinger's a candidate for a public office. People he'd be representing have a right to know about potential conflicts of interest, and about past ones involving him and the person he wants to replace."

Mr. Braden nodded. "Stick to facts—which we've got plenty of, straight from the public record. No conclusions. And no paraphrasing anything Galinger said. Just straight quotes there."

Harrison hesitated. "We could wait a day—dig around and try to paint a more complete picture. Though . . ."

"Though if we do, someone else will beat us to the story," Mr. Braden said. "You want to waste an exclusive?"

"No," Harrison said. "I don't."

Fran said, "Me, neither. Besides, you can do more in a follow-up. You and Maggie will be on this one awhile."

CHAPTER 14

Harrison worked on the story all afternoon, and I made phone call after phone call, under his direction, checking and rechecking everything.

Along with Fran and Harrison and me, Mr. Braden read the page proof with the finished article.

It began, "Previously undisclosed financial ties between developer Ralph Galinger and a recently deceased Eastside city councilman who chaired the planning committee responsible for approving several Galinger Construction projects came to light this week when *Herald* reporters . . ."

The lead didn't mention which reporters, but it didn't need to. Above the story were the words "By Ed Harrison of the *Herald,* with contributions from Margaret Wynn Chen."

By then, other staffers had come over, their interest adding to a current of excitement that had been building all day. Everyone knew we had something that was more than routine.

Those standing close in, like Jillian, heard Mr. Braden thump the page proof and say to Harrison and me, "Good work, you two."

She waited till the others had drifted away. Then she said, for once sounding sincere instead of ditzy, "That's great, Maggie. It's really cool that one of us has been able to work on a real story."

She pointed to the page proof that I was still reading. "And look! Your name's right there." Tapping the byline at the top, she said, "That is so, so . . ."

But I was looking at the last paragraph: "Any investigation into possible improprieties in city planning practices could further delay work already backlogged because of Yeager's death and the abrupt resignation of planning office employee Donald Landin shortly thereafter. Landin was subsequently killed in a drive-by shooting near the International District May 23."

The International District? I'd assumed the shooting had occurred on the Eastside. That since he'd worked there, that was probably where he'd lived.

"Harrison," I said. "Is that right? About where Landin was killed?"

"Yeah, in front of his apartment," he said. "Does it matter?"

"No," I answered. "Except that's where my dad died—or in the same area, anyway—that afternoon."

Frowning, Harrison said, "Could he have been chasing the same story?"

"Since he covered business news, I suppose it's possible," I replied. "Only I think his boss would have said so."

"Well, it's easy enough to check," Harrison said. "Someone can call him tomorrow. I'll mention it to Fran. And meanwhile, you ought to give yourself a pat on the back. If your father *was* going after the Galinger story, he'd have been pleased that you found the connection that brought it in!"

I went home brimming with details of the piece that would be in the next morning's paper. The evening before, I'd given Mom only the bare outline of what Harrison and I had been working on. Now, though, I had an actual story to tell her about, and it was one with my name attached to it. Not a byline, exactly, but clear acknowledgment that I'd helped. I might have worked all summer without something like that happening.

"Mom, you should have heard Galinger. He's the developer who . . ." I rattled on a bit and then stopped short. If Mom was excited for me, she sure wasn't showing it.

"What?" I asked. "Is something wrong?"

"I just wish you were doing something else with your summer," she answered. "Having a good time. Playing and going places with your friends."

"Bett and Aimee are in the San Juans," I reminded her. "A ferry ride and fifty miles away. And this is better than playing. It's doing a real job that's important. What if somebody's building a house on land that won't support it, because an elected official took a payoff to—"

Mom busied herself pulling salad makings from the refrigerator.

"Mom!" I said. "I want to tell you about this. It's really a big deal."

Her face tightened, and the cords in her neck strained taut. She set out a cutting board and washed a tomato. Then she turned to me. "I know. And I want to hear. It's just hard."

"Why?"

"Because you sound so much like your father. Because you *are* just like him."

She continued making salad, shredding lettuce, slicing a cucumber. Chopping green onions so fast it sounded like mahjong tiles clicking.

Then she said, "I'm sorry, Maggie. That was selfish. I'm proud of you and your story. I only wish you'd stay a kid a while longer. I'm not ready to lose you, too."

"It's just a job, Mom."

"The internship is. But the news? I know you as well as I knew your father, and that means knowing it can consume you." She managed a small laugh. "Not to be melodramatic."

I laughed with her. "Not to worry. I have another year of high school, and I promise to enjoy it."

But as I set out place mats and water glasses, I went back over what she'd said, focusing on a different part from what she'd meant me to. Her words reminded me about Dad's unknown family, and how I'd decided to find it for myself. Despite how my work at the *Herald* had made him feel close, the Galinger story had driven that project from my mind.

Friday, I thought. *I'll be off.* I could get back to it then. At least start brainstorming how I might find a record of one boy in all California.

Unless, of course, things were breaking so fast on the Galinger front that maybe Harrison would need my help. If they were, Fran might let me work an extra day, since it was my story, too.

"What are you smiling at?" Mom asked.

"Nothing. Just thinking."

Actually, I was picturing the next morning's paper. I would get it from the front door. Unfold it. See right there in print the same words thousands of other people were seeing: "with contributions from Margaret Wynn Chen."

That, at least, would tell the world one undeniable fact about who I was. I was someone who had helped find the lies and the truth behind a story.

FAI-YI LI, 1934

Li Dewei takes me with him the day he goes to meet his family at the docks, so that I can help with their belongings. We go to a ship, where we watch people stream off, but we cannot get close enough for him to pick out his wife from the others who plod toward the reception center that Sucheng and I went through.

"There will be many questions," I tell him. "It may take a long time."

"That is all right," he says. "I will tell the authorities I am here, and then I will wait."

Still, I am the one who waits outside the building for hours and hours. And when Li Dewei finally emerges, he carries his small son in his arms and there is no woman with them. In silence we return to the laundry, where he leaves the child before going back out, somewhere.

"His wife got sick on the ship. She died a week away from land," I tell my sister.

Sucheng shrugs. "How soon do we leave?"

"Not today! Li Dewei needs our help."

The little boy, whose American name is Philip, tugs on her. He is so young his walk is still unsteady, and I tell myself that surely she must see that Li Dewei cannot care for him alone.

She keeps asking, though, day after day, and her pestering irritates me.

"There is no hurry," I tell her more than once, watching the angry gestures with which she changes little Philip's soiled clothing or pulls him from the stove.

And finally I lose patience. "If you did not wish this life, you should have thought better when you demanded to come to America!"

My voice is harsh, covering the truth that more and more I am glad to be here. And covering, too, my regret that I have not found a safe way to let our parents know where we are and why we left.

Besides, I tell myself, she should see that her life is not so confined now that she has a household to care for.

In the early morning she goes out, buying food from the vegetable stands that line the streets and from meat and fish shops where chickens hang in windows and shining salmon lie on tables in overlapping waves. And all day she has little Philip to keep her company.

Some days I have company, also.

For by now Li Dewei has needed more medicines, and An and I have had more occasions to talk. And some late afternoons I go out even when there is no errand to do, and Li Dewei does not ask why, as long as my work is done. He appreciates that I am trying to learn the ways of my new country, and perhaps he thinks that is my intent.

But I go to meet An, as often as she lets me know that a meeting is possible.

Because now, when she walks by with her girlfriends, sometimes there is a quick nod—no more—a nod that means Meet me.

Li Dewei is too preoccupied to notice. And if my sister, bringing in a bundle of folded shirts, Philip hanging on her clothing, happens to see, what does it matter? She cannot stop me from going out. An is no concern of hers.

And if I do not understand why An should wish to be with me, if only for the fifteen or twenty minutes that she can slip away unnoticed, that does not matter, either. It is enough that she does.

We have found a small lot where no one but a few old men go, and we sit on the far side, sheltered by a tangle of wild shrubbery so they cannot spot us and then tell her father.

The first times we go there, I worry that we will have nothing to talk about, but after that I worry that our short visits will never provide enough hours for all we have to say. An has so many questions, and she helps me find the words to answer them so that she can know what I know.

She asks about my home in China, and I tell her about lying awake listening to the pigs and chickens of the family next door, who seemed not to be aware—not the people nor their animals—when daylight was done.

She wants to know how the days went in my village, and I tell her how a man as strong as two men sweated to turn the huge stone that ground corn.

She wants to know about my voyage coming over—what the ocean looked like and if I think I will ever go back.

"Cold and big," I tell her. "Yes, if I can. At least, that is what I think."

And then I say, "Now you talk to me," and she tells me about something that has happened at school, or about some funny person who has visited her father's shop. Sometimes I listen to the words and sometimes only to the music of her voice saying them. And if I ask questions, sometimes it is because I want her stories to go on.

One day she throws up her hands, laughing, and says, "I can think of no more to tell you."

I tell her, "Then say the same thing again. I will enjoy it as much."

If I dared, I would touch the pink that rises in her cheeks.

Another day she brings two photographs to show me. "Since you want so many stories," she says, "and since I have no more of my own!"

She tells me the man in the first photograph is a relative who came to this country, but to San Francisco, a long, long time ago, and who has been dead a long time, also. He has a goatee, he wears a satin coat and a round satin hat, and he sits very straight in a heavily carved chair.

"He was a merchant," An says, and I think he does look like a man of wealth.

The other photograph is of his wife. She also wears satin, and her still face bears no expression.

"This picture is all I know of her," An says, "except for one story, and it is this. It is said she came to this country from China as a bride when she was only sixteen years old. She saw the streets of San Francisco from the horse-drawn cab that took her to her new home above the store her husband owned. And what is significant about this is that she never saw those streets again. For the rest of her life she stayed inside those rooms above the store."

An waits for what I will say, but when I have no response, she says, "I asked my father once, 'Do you think that story is true?' I couldn't imagine it, a girl the age I am now, shut up inside a few rooms for the whole rest of her life. He told me to enjoy the story and be glad I'm young now."

Now I have a reply. I tease, saying, "I think you are just the right age for now."

‹ ‹ ‹

One day I tell An about little Philip trying to help me move a heavy washtub, and how I let him believe that he had. An says, "You care a lot for your little brother, don't you?"

"For Philip," I say, not wishing to lie, but not correcting her, either, because to her, I am Philip's brother. "Yes. He has become my shadow, even when I work."

"And Sucheng's, I suppose?" An asks. "She must love his company."

"They are together much," I answer, again threading between lie and truth.

Yes, he is her responsibility. No, she does not like it.

It is always so when I talk with An about my sister—wanting there to be nothing held back between An and me. Feeling that I must not diminish Sucheng.

So often I wish I could tell An how Sucheng was when we were growing up, when she was little. Petted and loved, in return she had scattered warmth like the sun.

And even more often I wish I could tell An about me—say that I am not Fai-yi Li at all, but Wu Fai-yi. I would trust her with knowing. But I think of Li Dewei and Sucheng and remember that the secret is not mine alone.

And for that reason, also, I cannot tell An of my gratefulness that Li Dewei more and more relies on me as if I were *his son. Nor can I tell her of my frequent arguments with Sucheng, who grows more strident with her demands to leave.*

One time, when Sucheng comes upon me practicing my writing, for I am learning to read and write my new language now, she knocks the pen from my hand. "You will never be American. As long as we stay here, you will be nothing but another Chinese!"

"I am Chinese," I tell her. "That would be true anywhere."

"I want to go to Los Angeles," she says. "Denver. Chicago. New York." She pronounces the names as she heard them said all that time ago, when we were children and America was only a story.

"Sucheng," I say gently, the way I speak to little Philip, "this is a good place."

"For you!"

' ' '

She is right. It is a good place for me.

I begin to pay my sister to do some of my work, besides her own, so that Li Dewei will have no cause to complain, though I am gone more and more. An asks me one time if my sister minds.

"No," I answer. "He does not pay her the wages he does me."

"That's not fair," An says. "If you are paid, she should be also."

I do not know what to answer. So many ideas An has about what is fair and what is not. About how girls should be regarded, and about the things that are all right for them to do.

She asks if I am not glad she is American. She says it makes her modern and able to decide for herself that it is all right for us to see each other alone.

But when, one day, I try to kiss her, she stops that quickly enough. She says she is too Chinese to be kissed by a boy who is not her husband.

The way she says it makes me smile and be glad all over again that she wishes to be with me. An causes me to smile much; and always, when I think of her, I am happy.

And I hope that perhaps one day she will allow me to hold her hand.

CHAPTER 15

Harrison's and my story ran on page 1 above the fold on Thursday morning.

Mom was making pancakes when I went into the kitchen—something she usually did only on birthdays—and the newspaper was on the counter by a vase with roses so freshly picked there were still dewdrops on the petals.

"Pretty impressive," she said.

"Harrison really wrote it."

"I meant you. Though the article is, too. I wish your father could be here to read it and to . . . well, to see you're carrying on just the way he would have hoped."

In the newsroom there were lots of "Good jobs!" and some friendly jibes about Harrison letting a high schooler do his work. And what would be our next exposé? Date swapping on prom night?

The teasing rolled off us. We had follow-up work to do, beginning with another visit to that Eastside city hall.

The mayor hadn't returned any of Harrison's calls the day before, and now he had his office giving out a "no comment" message. We planned to make an in-person effort to speak with him, and after that we were going to Galinger Construction in search of employees willing to talk.

We were on our way out when Fran called, "Harrison! Maggie! Wait!"

She came from Mr. Braden's office to meet us. "Both of you, sit down a sec."

Then, looking at me, she said, "Sam Braden just talked to your dad's boss, who said that as far as he knew, your father wasn't working on anything local. But the coincidences between the two deaths are enough that once the police resume an active investigation into Landin's death—and they will now—they'll probably take another look at your dad's, too."

I nodded. "I figured that," I said. "I was thinking that Dad might even have been developing the story and just not told anyone yet. But what—"

"The thing is," Fran said, "it's going to give you a personal interest in what we report next. Which means we can't have you working on it."

"But—" I stopped, dismayed. How could she think of pulling me off a story that we might not have even had if I hadn't found the connection between Galinger and Yeager?

"Maggie," Harrison said, "Fran's right. If I'd stopped to think, I'd have reached the same decision."

It was hard to hold back tears. I managed to only because I knew that if I did cry, I'd never want to face anyone in the newsroom again.

And it was even harder to make myself say, "Sure. I understand."

Fran arranged for me to go to Lifestyles, and not alone. When I saw Jillian flounce over, I thought, *Don't let it be,* but it was.

Deena Craig, the editor in charge of that section, showed us to a table overflowing with envelopes addressed to "*Herald* Readers Cook!" "We didn't know what we were getting into, putting on a recipe contest," she said. "It will be a huge help if you girls would open and sort the entries by category."

She launched into instructions while I watched Harrison leaving the newsroom on his own. I saw others watch him leave and then look over at me, probably wondering why I wasn't with him.

"Any questions?" Deena asked.

"I guess not," I answered.

"Yeah, a few!" Jillian said once Deena had moved out of earshot. "Like, for starters, what is the point?" She ripped open an envelope. "Camp Delights? People need a recipe for s'mores? And from a newspaper?"

She tore into another one. "English muffin pizzas? Please!"

I grabbed a stack of envelopes and started sorting.

She went on. "I know why I'm here instead of with Lynch, who really needs me, despite that the doctor let him ditch his crutches and he can carry his own gear now. It's so I can make you feel better. About being pulled off your own assignment, I mean."

She scanned a recipe. "Buttermilk pie with a pecan crust. I'll mark this one 'Looks promising.'"

"We're supposed to be sorting, not judging," I told her.

"So we can't multitask? Anyway, I was saying that there is no way Lynch wouldn't rather have me working with him. He relies on me. I suggest camera angles, shots he hasn't thought of, sometimes even exposure settings. Not that he takes my advice, probably because there's some professional pride involved. But I've caught him listening once or twice. Actually, one time yesterday he did explain *why* he was going with his own settings, and it made sense."

The sorted piles grew higher while Jillian babbled on.

"Working with Lynch has given me a whole new outlook. Did you ever think, Maggie, just how much information a good photographer can pack into one picture? Or, I suppose, how much information a bad photographer can pack in, if he gets lucky? The point is, it's true that a picture is worth a million words."

"Jillian! Thousand!" I said. "The saying is 'A picture is worth a thousand words.'"

She frowned only momentarily. "That was probably from when we had lower resolution cameras. Anyway, what I think . . ."

After lunch, the Metro staff disappeared into the conference room with Fran, and I wondered what new developments Harrison would report. I wished he'd at least come tell me if he'd talked to the mayor and Galinger's employees.

The staff meeting broke up when a tanker truck collision on one of the floating bridges sent the environmental reporter and a photographer running for their cars. Jillian and I knew only because a local television station carried the scene live. I thought that—probably for the first time—she and I were thinking exactly the same thing. What good was being in a newsroom if you got your news from a TV?

And then in midafternoon Tonk came over and set a large Starbucks cup in front of me.

"From Sports," he said. "We know you don't do coffee, so it's a white hot chocolate steamer, with some caramel and hazelnut added. Jake says to tell you congratulations on the story this morning, he's sorry you had to be pulled off it, and if you want back on Sports, he'll beg Fran for you."

Jillian, returning from the women's restroom just then, asked, "How about me? Latte? A job offer?"

Tonk looked at her blankly and then said, "Sorry. We didn't even think. Because Maggie's kind of one of ours . . ."

"Go," Jillian said. "I'm teasing."

As soon as he was gone, she took a long pull on the steamer. "You know," she said, "he's kind of cute. Too old, but cute. You want some?" She pushed the drink over. "So do you have a boyfriend?"

I shook my head.

She took the drink back.

"I meant, no, I don't have a boyfriend," I said, pulling the cup back to me.

"Oh! Well, it's a little on the sweet side, anyway. Not any? Not ever?"

"I didn't say that," I answered, my voice a bit sharp, but I was annoyed. "I had a boyfriend where I lived before, but we broke up when I moved here. Which was okay. I'd outgrown him." I felt myself flush with embarrassment. "Not that I'm so perfect," I added. "But he didn't know how to be serious."

Jillian planted both hands on the table and studied me intently. And then she announced, "Don't get me wrong, but maybe you come on a little *too* serious. I mean, take that outfit you're in."

Not wanting to wear all my new things one after another, I was back in my linen pants and Mom's cream-colored shirt.

"Boring!" Jillian said. "Maybe it was okay the first day, when you wanted to make an impression, but everything you wear says business. It's no wonder you don't have a boyfriend."

"I did. I will again. And the old one didn't break up with me," I said. I couldn't believe I was defending myself, but I couldn't make myself stop, either. "It was a mutual thing."

I thought, *Please, just let this day end.*

Though, of course, I knew it wouldn't, not for another two long hours in which I wouldn't have any peace to think about what Harrison might be learning or about whether Dad might have gone after the same story on his own.

I made myself focus on my work, looking again at several entries I'd been undecided about. "'My grandmother's recipe for borscht, from the old country,'" I murmured, reading the note on one. Did it belong with Main Dishes, Soups, or From Foreign Lands?

"And how does she know her grandmother didn't get it from a cookbook?" Jillian asked. "Maybe that's what she thinks—"

"He," I said, wanting to strangle myself for reading out loud. "A man sent it in."

"So *he*. My point is, he's just telling you what he believes, but he could be wrong. Or he might know it's from a cookbook but think we won't find out. Everyone lies sometimes, don't they? Even the most honest people?"

Finally five o'clock came. Or rather, almost five. Jillian grabbed her bag, a large, brightly embroidered drawstring affair, and announced, "I'm out of here."

There were only a few contest entries left. I dealt with them, straightened the piles, and asked Deena if there was anything else she wanted me to do.

"No," she answered, "you did just what we needed." Then, spotting something under the table, she bent down and pulled out a wallet. "Yours?" she asked, and when I shook my head, she looked at the driver's license inside. "Jillian's."

"It must have fallen from her bag."

"And by now she's on her way home, probably not even realizing she's driving without a license." Deena read the address. "I'd drop it by, but it's in the opposite direction from where I have to pick up my kids."

I wanted so much to say it was in the opposite direction for me, too, or that I had someplace I had to be. But a lie was a lie, and despite what Jillian thought, not everybody told them. At least not when they didn't have to.

Although it was the last thing I wanted to do, I said, "I'll take it. It's on my way."

CHAPTER 16

Jillian lived in a multi-building apartment complex, down a dusty-floored hall that smelled of food and could have used some fresh paint. A woman with her hair in a ponytail too young for her face answered my knock.

"Jilly's wallet!" she exclaimed, pulling me inside. "Now, you just come in and wait so she can thank you herself. She's gone for a burger, but she'll be right back."

As Mrs. Smythe moved about the apartment, her voice faded in and out over the sound of running water, clothes hangers jangling, and the *snap-snap* of containers of makeup.

Coming back into the living room to put on a pair of sturdy tie shoes, she said, "I'd stay and visit, except I've got a boss who'll dock you for being a few minutes late. Can you imagine? Docking somebody for ten minutes off an hour he's only paying minimum wage for anyway? And then acting like tips are skin off his nose, when he's not the one balancing trays and trying not to slip on french fries some kid's thrown on the floor. If it weren't for Jilly, I'd tell him what he could do with his job."

She sounded so exactly like Jillian I was afraid I'd start giggling, despite knowing that what she was saying wasn't funny at all. A scarred coffee table held a few magazines, and to cover my confusion, I reached for them. There was a *Cosmopolitan,* an old issue of *People*—and, under those, a literary journal with a bookmark in it.

Mrs. Smythe, who was piling things into a shoulder bag, said, "They printed something of Jilly's. Can you imagine? She's quite the little writer, though too somber, if you ask me. I like a story that's fun and takes your mind off things, the way sitting down takes a load off your feet. I tell her, 'Now, if you'd just write the way you talk!' But I suppose you don't listen to your mother, either. I know I didn't when—"

Just then Jillian came in, saying, "Hey! I've lost my wallet!" Then she saw me. "Oh!"

"You dropped it at work," I said. I stood to go, but Mrs. Smythe gave me a little push down.

"Jilly will get some lemonade—I just mixed some—and then the two of you can curl up for a nice chat. Jilly, you make your friend welcome. It's high time you had someone in."

In the sudden quiet after Mrs. Smythe left, Jillian and I just looked at each other for a moment. Then Jillian, her voice oddly subdued, said, "You don't need to stay. But if you want to, you can. I mean, I'll get the lemonade. Or there's probably iced tea, or—"

"I ought to go home," I said. "Although, first—" I gestured to the journal I'd put back on the coffee table. "Your mom said you have a piece in this. May I see it?"

Taking her shrug to mean yes, I turned to "Girl on a Doorstep," by Jillian Smythe.

Her canted eyes stare vacantly and her too-full lips hang slack. Only her right hand moves, fingers scratching across the concrete doorstep where she sits. She's long since become invisible to the boisterous, sullen, arguing, joyous packs of kids who pass by.

She waits for the big girl with the swirling skirts who sometimes stops to sit beside her. They talk with a torrent of words that cross between them on spit and air . . .

"Wow!" I said, looking up. "You packed a lot into that opening."

"You think it works?" Jillian asked.

"It's a picture."

"A picture is what I was going for," she said in a tone that sounded as though for once she was saying something she'd actually thought about. "Only I'm wondering now if I might have done it better with a camera. Like Lynch does."

But then she began blathering on, the way she usually did.

"A thousand words and all. Not a million. I remember. Though, really, it's not like a person can say *Here's a 1,030-word photo,* or *That one's worth just nine hundred and eighty.*"

Tuning her out, I read the rest of the piece and then on impulse said, "That girl's you, isn't it? The older girl. Unheard behind all that talk."

Jillian's eyes widened with a *caught* look. But then she laughed. "No way. You should try writing fiction sometime. I mean, sticking to facts can be such a pain, even though there are places, like the newspaper, where—"

"Jillian! Stop!" I said. "Just . . ."

I almost left without finishing my thought, which was that I wished she'd shut up rather than ruin the spell cast by her writing.

But maybe because of what she'd written, I didn't leave.

I told her, "If you can write like that, if you can see things that way, then you ought to let people know. You don't have to go around disguising yourself as a total airhead."

Her face told me I'd gone too far, and I braced myself for a stinging retort. I was sure she was framing one. But then, looking unexpectedly vulnerable, she asked, "Do you think Lynch would laugh if I told him how much I like photography? If I promised to stop talking and to listen, if he'd just keep me on and teach me some?"

"He might laugh," I said. "But he might take you at your word, too. I think you should take a chance."

She studied me a moment before saying, "Maybe I will. Now I'll get us the drinks and you can tell me your secrets. Or don't you have any?"

"Not really," I said, but that made me feel guilty, because she'd been honest with me.

I began telling her that I'd embarked on a genealogy project, making it sound like I'd taken it on as a way to remember my father. But it was such a relief to finally be talking to someone, I ended up telling her the truth. I wanted to find his birth family because they were my family, too, and different from the one I'd always thought I belonged to.

"Telling it, it doesn't sound very important," I said. "Lots of people don't even know their fathers, much less their father's family."

"It's important," Jillian said. "Even though they were made up, those people you believed in were a part of you. And now you must feel like you don't know yourself."

Which said so completely and exactly how I did feel that I couldn't respond.

"It must have hurt when you found out your father lied to you," Jillian said. "But I bet he had a really good reason."

And then, suddenly, we both seemed to know it was time to stop talking.

We promised to keep private what we'd said, and I walked to my car not sure why I'd told Jillian, of all people, about Dad.

But at least I had one mystery solved. I now knew why the *Herald* had hired Jillian. She could write, and she had worthwhile things to say.

When I got home, I found a message from Mom stuck to the hall mirror. "Running errands. A casserole's in the oven. I'll be back by the time it's hot."

The house smelled of the basil tomato sauce Dad had loved, and for a few moments I let myself pretend that time had rolled back. That Dad would be coming home any minute, calling, *Where're my girls?* He'd have hugs for us both, and pieces of a world bigger than ours would be clinging to him.

I wandered through the house, wanting, missing, wishing things could somehow turn back to the way they'd been. Before secrets. Before wondering. Before anything—anybody—had gone missing.

I rested my hand on the back of his favorite reading chair. Touched a geode he found the summer we tried rock hounding. Stopped in the hall to examine a photo I took of him and Mom the day we explored Puget Sound by ferry. I knew in my heart it was a true picture that said how much Dad loved all the good times we'd had together.

I suddenly thought about Jillian, always putting herself so *out there,* seeming to say whatever clueless thing came into her mind but never mentioning her writing, or how she saw the world in pictures. All that chatter just to keep private—maybe protect—the serious, mattering things inside her.

And I thought about Dad. Could that be why he'd made up a story about himself? To protect something too fragile to risk sharing?

And if so, what?

CHAPTER 17

Mom was still in the kitchen, about to leave for school, when I got up the next morning. "You look happy," I said.

"Starting Chaucer in my survey class, and I think I may have some students who'll appreciate him! What are you up to?"

"I'm going to enjoy my day off, though I'll pay the bills first."

"I've got them set up for you."

While eating breakfast, I paged through the newspaper till I found Harrison's follow-up to the Galinger story. It was short, and the only new thing in it was a statement from the mayor. Apparently he'd decided his original *no comment* stance hadn't cast him or his city in a good light.

"We have a fine town run by a hard-working, honest government," Harrison quoted him saying, "and I'm certain that when all the facts come out, you'll find there's not been a breath of wrongdoing. But meanwhile, I want the citizens to know that my office will cooperate fully with any official investigation into any alleged possible improprieties."

Still smiling at the qualifications—*alleged, possible*—I started in on the work I'd told Mom I would do.

Using a couple of the signed checks she'd left me, I paid the utility and garbage companies. I paid the phone bill and made a note to ask Mom if we should go to a cheaper plan. Without Dad making calls, we had hundreds of unused minutes.

Bills done, I read through several text messages from Bett and Aimee and sent a long e-mail answer back. "Yes, my job is going better. Mostly. Yes, I am getting along better with the other intern. Yes, I do wish I was in the San Juans, at least today, which I have off. Some fun with no unsettling questions would be really nice."

I deleted that last sentence so they wouldn't call asking *What unsettling questions?* and sent it off.

And then, with all that behind me, I turned to the bigger task I'd set myself: trying to track down Dad's high school.

I'd been mulling it over, and I had a plan. Mr. Ames said he was sure that Dad was from a city, because he had street smarts. That sounded like a big city to me. So I'd start with the biggest, Los Angeles, and work down.

And I'd call only public schools, since if Dad had been as short on money as Mr. Ames said, a private school probably wasn't likely.

I thought fleetingly of the letter Mom had received from the private eastern prep school Dad had *not* attended: the letter that had started everything. Maybe a public school wouldn't even have written.

I didn't finish with Los Angeles till after lunch, and by then I was thinking my plan could use revising, if I could just figure out how.

But then I got lucky. On my third San Francisco call I

reached a new clerk who was eager to help and was befuddled by the workings of the school's computer system. "It's all being redone," she said, "and all I know is I'm not supposed to type anything into anything that might change anything."

"I don't want you to," I said. "I'm just trying to find the high school my dad graduated from, probably in 1978. If you could just check . . ."

Within moments she read Dad's name back to me.

"If you'll tell me how to get in touch with any teachers who might remember him, I'd like to talk to them," I said.

"I don't know the teachers yet, since it's vacation. And anyway, probably I'd have to get their permission to give you their names. Because of privacy, I mean. Actually, I don't know if I should have even—"

"It's okay," I said. "You've been great."

Thanks to working with Harrison, I didn't have to think twice about what to do next. I went online, where I learned that the clerk's worry about privacy wasn't shared by the school's alumni association. It had posted entire sections of several yearbooks, including the one from Dad's senior year.

There was his name, "Steven Chen," under a photo in which he looked very young but was definitely Dad. But it was the text under his name that got to me. "Does anyone know this person? Newspaper. National Honor Society. Lives in library. Knows all the world's capitals. Ambition: to be a writer. Biggest distinction: invented the word *loner.*"

What a snarky, mean, backhanded blurb, I thought, angry and aching for him at the same time. No wonder Dad had wanted people to think he'd had a life different from the one he'd really had.

But a loner? My dad?

If it weren't for the picture, I'd think I had the wrong Steven Chen.

I stroked Pepper's head and replayed in my mind all I'd learned. I didn't want Dad to have had an unhappy past. Not the dad I'd known and not the stranger dad, either.

Then I called Bill Ames once more, reaching him just as he got home from work.

I apologized for bothering him again. "But I wondered—did Dad have a good time in college? Have people to hang with?"

For several moments there was silence on the line. Then Mr. Ames said, "You remind me of him, wondering about the strangest things. But to answer you, I don't think so, not real friends. Though I sometimes thought Steven was trying to learn how to make them."

"And no girlfriends, either?" I asked.

"Just one that I knew of, for a brief time our senior year. He fell hard for her and was shocked when she broke things off. Crushed, too."

"Do you remember why she did?" I asked.

"He didn't tell me. Just said he'd always wonder if they were meant to be together and if she'd left before they had a chance to find out."

By the time I got off the phone with him, I had so much churning through my mind. Strands I wanted to pull out and think about. Questions I wanted to ask Mom.

And thoughts I wanted to tell her, too, like . . . like that I was glad she'd loved Dad.

I pictured her going to school that morning, eager to teach Chaucer. Dad used to tease about having to share her affections with a writer dead for six hundred years, who wasn't even Chinese.

One time he'd added, "But I can live with the competition. It's April. The weather's fine, and Maggie and I are taking off for the afternoon."

Before we left, he set things up for Mom to celebrate spring lounging in our hammock under sweet-smelling trees in blossom, drinking iced tea, and listening to a recording of the *Canterbury Tales.*

Her "When in April" day had become a tradition, like my ocean birthdays.

Dad knew her so well, I thought. And they'd loved each other so much it had been almost embarrassing.

Now I was glad they had, I thought, as I considered where my search might go next.

I'd already made more progress than I could have reasonably hoped for in one day. Now I'd have to find out who to contact to learn more. Figure out how to approach them, because if I did it wrong, I'd be told individual files were private. But I had something solid to go on now: a school and attendance years. That had to be a key to a lot.

But it was still too overwhelming—the school yearbook

and what Mr. Ames said—for me to return to the computer and start right in again.

Instead I turned on the television and flipped through channels. I stopped at the 4:00 p.m. news because I heard my high school mentioned—some of the streets near it were being designated one-way.

Short items followed: a grocery store in violation of health codes, proposed restrictions on lawn watering. And then there was a fast summary of the Galinger story, along with the additional information that Ralph Galinger was wanted by authorities for questioning.

"Also," the piece ended, "police have intensified their investigation into the shooting death of Planning Department employee Donald Landin and are looking at possible connections to the hit-and-run killing of journalist Steven Chen."

Hearing Dad's name broadcast like that made me bite my lip so hard I drew blood.

I wished I'd never pointed out that Dad's death happened close to where Landin died, and on the same day. Maybe nobody would have noticed.

Besides, it really didn't matter now whether Dad had been in the International District area because he'd become lost avoiding traffic, the way police figured, or because he was working the Galinger story himself. Knowing wouldn't bring him back.

What made me angry was the careless way the TV news people had worded the story. "Connections." That made it sound like Dad was a suspect in the crime.

They should have made it clear that investigators were just

interested in knowing whether he was there because he was a working reporter. Where did the TV people get off using a loaded word like *connections*? Dad had covered crimes sometimes. But he didn't connect to them, get entangled in them, become involved.

Not my Dad, who was honest as . . .

I started to phone the *Herald* but got my car keys instead. I was more likely to get answers if I asked my questions in person.

CHAPTER 18

After a frustratingly slow beginning-of-rush-hour drive later, I got to the newspaper. From the lobby I could see that Harrison wasn't at his desk, and I asked the receptionist if she knew whether he was in the building.

She told me, "I saw him go downstairs not long ago."

I found him coming out of the business office, muttering about a messed-up paycheck. "But what are you doing here?" he asked.

"I came to see you. The TV news had something about Galinger, and the way they talked about Dad . . . What's going on?"

"You shouldn't be here," Harrison said. "You're off the story."

"I know," I told him, and I waited.

Finally, looking reluctant, he said, "Some of it will be in tomorrow's paper anyway. Investigators going through Yeager's bank records found the payments to Landin. The checks were made out to cash, but Yeager had noted 'Plan. Dept.' on the copies, and the amounts tied to deposits in Landin's bank account."

"So?" I said. "That just backs up what we guessed."

Harrison looked away for a moment before meeting my eyes again. "Yeager didn't write many checks for cash, and the only other large one in recent months had the notation 'News' on the copy. Which opens up the possibility that someone in the news media was aware of what Yeager and Galinger were doing and was taking money to cover it up."

"You mean, like a bribe. Or blackmail."

"One or the other."

"But they don't know who?"

"No."

As the potential meaning of that hit me, I felt the blood drain from my cheeks. My dad, mixed up with Yeager and Galinger? *Impossible.*

"And so," I said, "because Dad was a reporter, instead of thinking he might have been working, everyone's assuming—"

"Not everyone. And not assuming," Harrison said. "Considering."

Impossible, I thought again.

Maybe Dad had lied about his family. Lied about who he was, even to Mom and me. Maybe he'd lied about other stuff, too. There was still one thing I knew without a doubt.

"My father would not have taken a bribe or blackmail over a story," I said. "He cared about journalism too much." I paused, needing Harrison to understand. "Being a newsman was who Dad *was.*"

Again I halted for a moment, realizing I'd said something important that I'd need to examine, but not right then.

"And besides," I went on, "he was a hundred percent honest about money. One time I bragged about a store giving me a dollar too much in change, and he made me return it and apologize."

Harrison smiled, though he looked serious, too. "You don't have to sell me," he said. "I believe you."

"But what can I do?" I asked.

"Wait it out. When Galinger's picked up, one of the first things he'll be asked is the identity of anyone Yeager paid off."

"And if Galinger doesn't say? Or—"

I bit down on my lip, reopening the cut where I'd bitten down earlier. "Or what if he doesn't know? What if this person never gets caught?"

Harrison didn't answer, but he didn't need to.

"Then," I said, "the possibility that Dad was corrupt might hang out there forever. And when people think about Dad, that's what they'll remember. That's not right."

"No," Harrison agreed. "That's the worst thing about the news. Totally innocent people sometimes get hurt."

I stared at him, feeling helpless and remembering that he'd said that before. The thing was, before, we hadn't been talking about my father.

Mom came home still happy about teaching Chaucer, so I knew she hadn't heard the news.

"We need to talk," I said, following her into the living room. "You remember the story I was working on earlier this week?"

"The corruption scandal. Of course," she said, settling into a chair. "What about it?"

"Dad's name has come up. It's because his accident happened not far from where the Planning Department employee was shot, and on the same day."

Mom paled as she took that in. "Do they think your father was working on the story?"

"It's a possibility," I said. "I think the police will look into a lot of angles, and—"

I didn't know how to get started. Driving home after talking to Harrison, I'd realized I couldn't keep Dad's secret any longer. If investigators focused on Dad, there was no telling what they might learn and ask Mom about. And I didn't want her blindsided.

"I think," I finally said, "if police do go poking into Dad's affairs, they may find an identity issue. Regarding who his parents were—and some other stuff."

Mom regarded me as though she wondered if I was losing my mind. "Whatever are you talking about? Your grandmother and grandfather Chen were his parents. You know that."

"I *thought* I knew it," I said. "But . . ."

And then slowly, trying to give Mom time to absorb each piece, I explained about reading his notes and then about all the phone calls I'd made. "So Dad really was from a different family than—"

"That's preposterous," she broke in. "Even more ridiculous than that prep school letting its computer lose track of him. And, I'll point out, you got that mistake corrected."

"Mom," I said, "that's not *exactly* what I told you. I just said the school's records are right now."

"Don't mince words with me. Where is this notebook you read? I want to see it."

I wanted to cry with frustration at her and at myself and at how stupid I'd been, throwing Dad's notes away. "I don't have it anymore," I said. "But what I've said is true, and you need to think about what the police might find if they do start investigating Dad."

This time she heard the other half of what I was saying. Looking at me incredulously, she demanded, "Why would they . . . You're not suggesting they think your father might have been involved in anything illegal? That is absolutely the most outrageous—"

"I don't know what they think," I said. "But I know you need to believe me."

"Well, I don't. And I've no idea what's come over you, to make all this up."

"I'm not making anything up," I said. "Just—"

I tried to guess when the lies might have started for her. "Tell me about getting to know Dad."

"That has nothing to do with—"

"Please," I said.

Finally she said, "You've heard it before. I was teaching high school in the Texas town where I grew up, and he moved there to take a job on the newspaper."

"But how did you actually meet?" I asked. "Did someone introduce you? Or set you up for a date?"

"No. He came out to the school to cover a drama club production I had been in charge of."

"Did you have any common friends who knew him before he moved to town?"

"Of course not. He was from up north."

"And later on," I continued, "why did you elope instead of having a regular wedding?"

"Oh, for heaven's sake!" Mom exclaimed. "We wanted to get married, not put on a party. And Steven's parents were no longer living. He said a wedding without them would have made him sad."

The corner of Mom's mouth had begun twitching, and I felt awful for what I was doing to her. But I couldn't see a choice.

"Mom, the corruption story is out there and expanding."

"A story you helped with!" she said.

"Yes, and I wish I hadn't, because I'm afraid Dad's going to get caught up in it. Actually, because I'm afraid he already is."

By now Mom was holding herself so rigidly that her body trembled. "I don't want to hear any more. And don't tell me I don't know who my husband was!"

She punched the padded arm of her chair. "Don't tell me!" she said. And then, "I won't have it!" Her eyes glistened with tears. "Whatever you think you've found out, forget it."

And then she hit the chair again. "I won't have it! I won't."

CHAPTER 19

Later that night, I lingered in the hall outside her room. "I'm sorry," I said. "I never should have kept things secret from you. But at first I thought that if no one else knew, it would be like I didn't, either. And then—"

Mom waved away the rest of what I wanted to tell her: how I'd decided I wanted the truth for myself. Her voice husky, she said, "It's been a long day. Go to bed."

"I didn't make any of it up," I said. "You can call the high school yourself. And talk to Mr. Ames."

"No more," Mom said. "Just go to bed."

Later still, looking up into darkness, I thought again how stupid I'd been tearing up Dad's notes. If I hadn't, at least I'd have had them to show to her.

Though I didn't know what good that really would have done. It wouldn't have answered all the questions he'd left behind. Questions that stretched back decades. Questions from the day he got killed.

I wanted to believe there were good answers for all of them, and I did believe there was a good explanation for what he was doing by the International District that afternoon—one that had nothing to do with taking part in anything wrong.

I just wanted the explanation to be something more provable than a guess he'd gotten lost. A reason that had nothing to do with Donald Landin.

Suddenly understanding some of how Mom had felt hitting that chair arm, I sat up, grabbed a pillow, and hurled it across room as hard as I could. It thumped on the wall behind my dresser, and I heard something fall and then glass break. My framed picture of Dad with Mom and me.

I grabbed the other pillow and hurled it at my closet.

"Maggie?" Mom said from the doorway. "What's going on?"

"Nothing," I said.

The hall lamp cast a long rectangle of light on the pillows and broken picture on the floor.

Mom looked at them a moment. Then she nodded and went back to her room.

Much, much later I reached down to pet Pepper, asleep on her cushion beside my bed.

"What do you think, pup?" I whispered to my old friend, who could hardly be further from her puppy days. "Why did Dad tell the first lie, letting Mom think he'd come from a well-off family, when he hadn't? Because he was afraid of losing Mom the way he did that college girlfriend?"

I could understand that, and I could understand, too, how once that first lie was told, he'd have to maintain it.

But why had he let the story grow with prep schools? Museum boards? Family heirlooms like my jade ring?

Because each lie had led to a question that took a bigger lie to answer?

Pepper whined and nudged my hand so I'd keep on petting her.

"Yeah, that's also what I wonder, girl," I said. "After so many years, why did he go looking for the truth now, if that was really what he did?"

All I could do was guess.

Maybe his conscience had finally gotten to him. Perhaps at the banquet where he'd received that last award, all the praise for his integrity had laid on more guilt than he could stand.

Or maybe he'd just thought it was finally time when our family could survive the truth, provided the truth didn't turn out to be too awful. He and Mom were solid, and I was no longer a kid. *All's well with the Chens,* he'd signaled, driving away that last time we ever saw him.

Maybe he'd meant all was good enough that we could stand a rough bump.

I didn't fall asleep until almost dawn, and then it was into a nightmare of dark streets and screeching tires. I was a reporter getting a story, but then I wasn't. And it wasn't my father in the way of a hit-and-run driver, but me in the headlights of the onrushing car.

The lights got brighter and brighter, and I couldn't see who was driving. Or maybe I could. Maybe it was my father driving.

But then I saw that I was behind the wheel.

Driving and being run down at the same time. About to crash into myself.

And then I was at the *Herald,* sitting at a computer, having to report the whole story, and I didn't know where to start. I couldn't think of a lead sentence, couldn't even get my fingers moving on the keyboard.

FAI-YI LI, 1935

One day in another spring I pluck a white blossom and give it to An, an excuse to touch her hand. Her fingers entwine with mine—a familiarity no longer new, but it still fills me with wonder.

It is a familiarity that troubles An. Often we talk about the conflict she feels. At school she is a modern girl. At home she must be more like her mother and grandmothers were. And during the in-between hours, like these, she must decide how much of one and how much of the other she is.

Now, when I see An searching for words, I think she wishes to talk about this again. Instead she says, "My father is sending me away. As soon as I graduate here, I'm to begin a nursing program in California."

Heaviness fills me and then washes out, leaving me cold and hollow. I manage to say, "I did not know that was your plan."

"My father enrolled me."

"And it is not what you wish?" I ask.

"No."

She looks so sad, as desolate as I feel, that I would put my arms around her if it were not more than she permits.

"What do you want?" I ask.

"I don't know," she answers. But I feel her hand tighten around mine. "I want to be with you."

We sit so close that it almost causes me to forget I have brought her a present. It is a picture—a postal card—that shows the street on which she lives, though it is a photograph from an earlier year. "But it is not too old," I tell her. "Look there. You can see your father's shop."

I have inquired about the proper way to present such a card, and now, before giving it to her, I carefully write on the back, on three lines in one corner so I will not use up all the space, "With best regards, Li Fai-yi, Seattle." I am so intent on making each letter perfect that I do not see until too late I have put Li *first.*

"Oh!" I say. "I did not mean to do that."

"I like your name this way, too," she says. "Thank you for my gift." And then she starts laughing. "But—only best regards?" she asks. "That is all that comes with this gift?"

"No," I tell her. "Much more."

And although I do not say how much more, I believe she knows, for she no longer laughs. Instead she says, "Thank you, Fai-yi Li. I will keep your present always."

She will not hear that it is only a postal card and not worth such care.

But I know that if we can somehow have the time of years rather than of weeks and months, I will give her many more gifts, and they will be things of true value. Still, An, treasuring this small picture, makes me feel as though I have given her a jade carving set in gold.

* * *

Three weeks later I clean and brush my jacket and comb my hair smooth. Then I go as far as the arching entrance to An's school, and I wait.

And several hours later An is my wife and we are celebrating our wedding night. An has a few tears. "I thought more would be said," she tells me. "The official words were so few. And I feel so bad for my father. He must be frantic if he has not yet found my note."

I tell her, "We will go see him in the morning."

"No. I'd like to do that by myself," she says. "I need to make him understand."

"If that is what you want," I say, holding her now that I can. "But please do not be unhappy tonight."

Her answering smile tells me that mostly she is not.

* * *

An is up early the next day—much earlier than I would wish—saying she cannot sleep while the prospect of facing her father is before her. "I will not be long," she says. "And then I will come get you at the laundry, and we will talk with him together."

But she does not come for me, and finally I go to where her father's shop is and walk up and down the block, waiting for her to come out. There is a CLOSED *sign on the door, and the curtains in the upper-story windows are drawn.*

I watch a customer, annoyed at the sign, try the door anyway but turn away when he finds it locked.

And then a cab pulls up and An's father gets out, fumbles with a key, opens the door.

I hurry to him. "Where is An?"

He pulls me inside roughly, spilling out angry words. From the tumble of them I pick out a word that I have not heard before, but I know from the way he says annulled *that it is important.*

"What do you mean?" I ask.

"That this—mistake—never happened. You and my daughter are not married, and you were not."

I come to understand that he has seen officials and secured papers that make the marriage certificate given to An and me no good.

"But we are married," I say. "How can it be possible for you to undo such a thing?"

He does not bother to answer, and I wonder if he only had to tell the officials that he had not given permission. Or perhaps he paid money to someone to get what he wanted, the way I did to become Fai-yi Li.

"Now get out!" he says.

"Wait!" I say. "Please, listen! If you are worried how I will take care of An, I have thought of that. My father and I talked this morning of opening a second laundry that I will run."

I hasten to add, "Though, of course, I would not have An work in it. My sister would do that."

Mr. Huang makes a snorting sound. "Your father? Paper father! *You think I didn't guess?" he says. "An old customer of mine, needing money to bring over a wife and baby, suddenly acquires two almost-grown children that he has never before mentioned?"*

My heart pounds so hard that moments pass before I am able to ask, "Does An know?"

He doesn't have to answer. Of course he has told her.

"I can explain to her . . ."

"What? That you are so selfish you would take away who she is? An is not like me, still an alien, though I've been here since I was a baby. She was born here. A citizen. What if you were found out?" he demands. "Deported as an illegal? Do you not know that when a woman—any woman—marries a Chinese who is not a citizen, his status becomes hers?"

I struggle to absorb that. Is that really the law? Could he be lying? No. I can feel that he is not.

"Still, I must talk to her," I say.

"I've already sent her away, and you will not find her." He thrusts his chin forward. "Leave!"

I hardly see the streets and people around me as I walk the two blocks back to the laundry. All my awareness is inward, on questions of what An must be thinking and of where she might be. I am not willing to accept that I will never see her again.

*And I do not know what is best for her. Perhaps, if all her father has said is true, then the thing that is best is this word—*annulment.

But I will find her, and together we will decide.

‹ ‹ ‹

At the laundry, Sucheng, who has talked with Li Dewei, is waiting, rage on her face and venom in her voice. "What right have you to a wife? You owe me, me!"

She does not listen when I tell her what An's father has done. She hears only my concern for An.

"Do you think I care?" she demands. She sweeps her hand about, at the cramped, sweat-smelling shop. "You are not going to go off and leave me with this. It is not what I killed a man for!"

"Killed?" I repeat, uncomprehending. Then, "Oh, the man who died when you fought him off." Why is she dragging that up now, when I have so much more on my mind?

She looks at me with contempt. "How do you know his death was an accident?" she demands. "How do you know I did not lie in wait for him, and then for you to come by and find us. His dying did make you bring me here."

Again she sweeps her hand about the shop. "I hate you for not telling me how it would be."

But I hardly hear, because I am being pulled under to some place where pressure pushes in, squeezing on my chest, distorting all around me . . .

She is making this up, *I tell myself.* She is grabbing for a way to hurt.

I try to catch her in her lie. "The money," I say. "How could you know he would have enough money for us to come here?"

"Perhaps he did not," she answers. "Perhaps I took the money from our parents' safe earlier in the day and put it in his coat."

Her mouth curves. "Tell me you did not wonder about the money. Perhaps you did not ask these questions then because you also wanted to come to the Gold Mountain."

"No!" I say so loudly that Philip begins crying. "And . . . our parents! You must have taken all they had! How could you do that? Even think of doing it?"

She shrugs, but her hand comes up to her face.

And then, with blackness flooding though me, I grab her and shake and shake her until I feel as though there is nothing left inside me except bile going sour.

. . .

When Li Dewei comes in that evening, I do not have to tell him about Mr. Huang sending An away. "Mr. Huang is going, too," he says. "He is looking for someone to keep open his shop while he is gone."

"I have to find An," I tell him. "Can Sucheng remain here?"

And so that is what happens. I stay long enough to train a boy to work in my place while I am gone, and then I begin my search. At first I look close by, and then farther and farther away, to other cities, other Chinatowns, in Oregon and California.

I do not stop looking until I find someone in San Francisco who remembers meeting Mr. Huang. "It was many months ago," he tells me. "It was at the shipping office. He was purchasing passage to China for himself and his daughter."

"For a visit?" I ask.

"No. One way there," he answers. "I remember because I wondered what had made him so bitter that he would not want them to return."

After that I go back to Seattle and the laundry, and over time, as Li Dewei and I prosper, and as Philip grows up believing me to be his real brother, I settle into understanding that this is the life I have made.

. . .

I never do find a way to write my parents that would not mean putting onto paper names like Li Dewei's that are not mine to expose.

Many years later, though, after World War II ends, I travel to China once, along with many other Chinese Americans who also have served in the military. But unlike them, I do not go to bring back a bride. And not to find An, either, for even if it were possible, I would not break into her life again.

No, I go to find my parents and to try to right some of the wrong done them. If there was a wrong, beyond Sucheng and me leaving them with no children to carry on their name and care for them in their old age. For I never again speak to Sucheng of that long-ago death and how it happened. There is no reason to, when I cannot know whether anything she might say would be truth or lie.

And what can I say of my return to where I was born? It is to a country at war with itself, where there has been fighting of one kind or another for many years, and famine and more sickness.

The village where I grew up no longer exists except as the site of a huge factory. I can find no family in the surrounding countryside, and no one I talk with knows me or knows what has become of my parents.

And so, in the end, I walk toward the ocean, where I board another ship for America.

I can see the lonely years stretching out before me, like the endless gray swell of the sea. I can imagine there will be good things; perhaps Philip will have children and grandchildren who will call me Uncle. For their sake and for Li Dewei's, I make a kind of peace with Sucheng.

I am resigned to An's face fading from my memory. Already it has become hazy, like a face seen through oiled parchment.

What I do not foresee is that when I am very old and have lost my sight, hers will be the face I will see most clearly.

CHAPTER 20

The Galinger piece in Saturday's paper was short, saying mainly what I'd already learned from the television: that police wanted to question Galinger, who had disappeared. It also mentioned the reopened investigation into Dad's death, but only briefly. I could tell that Harrison had tried to walk a line between reporting the story honestly and giving Dad all possible benefit. But still . . .

I'd just read through it for a second time, feeling heartsick, when the phone rang. It was Jillian, who plunged right in.

"I saw the paper," she said. "I figured you'd be feeling awful."

"Pretty much."

"How's your mom taking it?"

"Hard. I had to tell her about Dad's—about the stuff I told you."

I paused and then said in a rush, "Jillian, it's such a mess—more than has been reported. And I'm so afraid that if things don't get cleared up, then years from now, whenever Dad's name is mentioned, somebody will say, *Steven Chen. Wasn't he involved in some scandal?* It's not something you want for your dad."

"Frankly," Jillian said, "my dad should have it so good. But I'm not calling about my absentee parent. I'm calling about yours, not that dead is exactly the same as absentee. But I've got an idea. You told me he'd been trying to find his birth family."

"I said I *thought* he might have been."

"Well, you're Chinese, right?"

"About a million generations back." I caught myself. "On Mom's side, anyway. I guess I don't know when Dad's people came here."

"My point is," she said, "have you considered that your father might have gone to the International District because he was looking for them there? The area used to be called Chinatown."

I told her it hadn't occurred to me because what I knew involved California. But . . . *possible search will end here?* Was it also because some unconscious part of me hadn't wanted a family search to lead to a place—to people—still foreign? I didn't want to think so.

I concentrated on what she was saying. If Dad had gone there hunting for family, it would be the reason I wanted, a reason that had nothing to do with Landin or the others, or with blackmail or bribes. And if I could find someone he'd talked to, I'd have proof.

"But how would I even start trying to find out?" I said. "I can't just go to hundreds, maybe thousands of doors, asking people if my father had been to see them. That's crazy."

"Hey," she said. "I didn't say I had answers for you. Just an idea. But if you do figure out what to do and want my help, call."

Right after I hung up, Mom came into the kitchen carrying empty canvas shopping bags. She pointedly ignored the newspaper. "I'll mail those bills you paid yesterday," she said. "Any problems with them?"

"No, except we can probably save some money on phone expenses. Dad must have done a lot more calling than we do."

"Part of his job," she said. "The wire service used to reimburse us for the business portion."

I promised to dig out our plan so we'd know what we could change.

Her comment had made something click, though, and once she was gone I got out the prior month's phone bill from among the business papers I'd dried and put away after the basement flood. It included the last couple of weeks that Dad had made calls, and it listed every one—the number, the place, how long.

And just as I'd thought, right there, about a week before he died, was a long stretch of calls to California. Ignoring only the very shortest, I went to work.

The first several calls got me nowhere except to unpromising machine messages or people who hung up or swore. The one man who did recognize Dad's name said, "Is this some kind of a scam? I told him I don't talk to strangers!"

And then I got hold of a woman who not only had talked to Dad but who said to me, "Oh, and it was good to hear from him. As though I could forget my little boy!"

My little boy! I almost didn't hear what she said next, I was so busy taking in the idea that I might have reached his mother. *My grandmother?*

I felt lightheaded for a moment, and dizzy with hope. Excited. In worrying over Dad, I'd almost forgotten this hunt was for me, too.

But then, as the woman kept talking, I realized she wasn't Dad's mom, but a woman who once ran a foster home and had taken care of him when he was in elementary school.

"He was sweet but so sad, and who could blame him?" she said. "All that nonsense about how people pull for underdogs—don't you believe it. Children can be cruel. And as for grownups . . . I wanted to shake some of the adults and say it wouldn't hurt you to invite these kids to a birthday party now and then, but they never did. Some of the kids who came here already had shells you couldn't get through, but not Steven. I'd go in to tell him good night and find him staring up at the ceiling, wanting to know why no one had adopted him. I used to call him my lonely heart."

I had to swallow back a lump in my throat before asking the other questions I'd called with.

She said that, yes, when Dad called her, it had been to find out if she could tell him anything about his past.

And no, she hadn't known anything to tell him.

She was glad he'd tracked her down, though, and she was very, very sorry to learn he'd died.

"But you sound like a nice daughter," she said. "I'm glad he finally got a family of his own."

I plowed through more California numbers. One got me to a department store and another to a man with a heavy accent—Russian, maybe—who'd never heard of my father. I was getting toward the end of the list when I called a San Francisco number.

A rough-voiced, older-sounding woman answered, "Yes?" In the background a car commercial blared.

She let me get only partway into explaining that I was calling about Steven Chen.

"Look," she said. "I told him I can't remember the doings of all the kids who ran through here. He was lucky I had a picture for him. I wouldn't of, if I'd remembered it when I packed him up."

"A photo?" I asked.

"What else? You hoped for something valuable? Kids like him don't have nothing valuable, and if they do, you can bet some agency worker's gonna make it disappear."

"But you kept the photo all these years?"

"In a drawer. Never got around to throwing it away."

And, I bet, never tried to send it to him, either, I thought, suddenly so angry for my dad's sake I could hardly talk. I willed my voice steady because I had to learn all I could.

"Please," I said, "would you just tell me about the picture? Was it someone's portrait?"

"No. Just a street. Some old Chinatown, it looked like."

"Was anything written on it?"

"Maybe. On the back. A little. I gotta go."

"Wait," I said. "Just tell me, did you mail it to him?"

"When he sent me an envelope with a stamp. I'm not a charity."

"And the words on the back. Do you remember any of them? It's really important."

"There was a name. *LO, LE,*" she spelled. "Something foreign. I'm missing my show," she said, and she hung up.

CHAPTER 21

A picture of an old-time Chinatown, I thought. I hadn't seen anything like that when I was sorting though the things from Dad's office. I had no faith that the woman had even sent it, stamped envelope or not.

Maybe it was a picture of San Francisco's Chinatown, since that's where she lived. But if it was, it wouldn't do me any good. I needed it to be Seattle. Or rather, I needed the name on the back to be a Seattle person Dad might have gone to see.

I wished I'd thought to ask the woman if there'd been a date.

I looked up both names in the phone book, locating the addresses on a map. There was only one Lo and no Le listings at all for within a few miles of where Dad got killed. Then I realized I might be spelling Le wrong, and checked Li and Lee. That gave me three possibilities.

I left a note for Mom in case she got home before I did: "Have some things to do in town. Will be back in time to start dinner." And then I got into my car and headed south.

Exiting I-5, I made my way through the International District and into an area of irregular blocks and construction detours. Becoming more and more confused as I drove, I pulled over twice to study the map I'd brought with me.

Finally, though, I got to the first place, only to find scattered bricks and debris where an old building had stood.

Mr. Lo, at the second address, thought I was a Meals on Wheels lady and threatened to report me if I didn't hand over his food. I escaped when the real one arrived, apologizing for being late.

An exchange student lived alone at the third place I drove to.

I got back in my car and went hunting for the last address, backtracking several times before finding the street.

Small older houses lined it, some with plastic toys spilling onto sidewalks. At a couple of places, added-on ramps provided wheelchair access.

The one I wanted was three blocks down, a neat brick home set apart from its neighbors by a garden that took up almost the whole yard. An old man was running a hose at the base of a rosebush laden with white blossoms. A boy on a ladder painted window trim.

Neither person turned around when I parked behind a pickup and got out, probably because the racket of a neighbor's power mower kept them from hearing me. Going up the short walkway, I called, "Hi!" and again, more loudly, "Hello!"

It startled the old man, who turned abruptly. A jet of water hit the cardigan I'd thrown over my shoulders, soaking one sleeve before my startled exclamation made him turn the hose away.

I started to protest and then saw his unfocused gaze searching for me. A long white cane lay by the edge of the garden. "I hope I did not hit you with the water," he said.

"I'm fine," I said, draping the wet sweater over a low fence. "Are you Mr. Li?"

"I am Fai-yi Li. And you? You sound like a young person."

He was even older than I'd first thought—perhaps in his nineties—and I could hear the trace of another language in his carefully enunciated words.

"I'm Maggie Chen. I'm still in high school," I said.

I hesitated, trying to frame the least awkward way to ask what I'd come to find out.

"I would like to know if my father, Steven Chen, visited you recently. He died in an accident near here a few weeks ago, and questions have come up that make it important to know why he was in this part of Seattle."

"Please accept my sympathy for your loss," Mr. Li said. "But I have had no visitors in quite some time. Certainly I did not know Mr. Chen."

Just then the painter, who appeared to be about my age, joined us. Glancing at the *Herald* parking decal on my car window, he said, "If you're selling newspaper subscriptions, my uncle doesn't want one."

"Ian," Mr. Li said, "this young lady's father died recently, and she came to ask if he had been here."

"Oh! Sorry! But why would he?"

"He was searching for information about his birth family," I said. "Or at least I think he was. He didn't have a lot to go on, but I think that just before his death he'd gotten a name. I'm not sure, but it might have been *Li*."

"As I have told you, that is my name," the old man said. "But I think your father must have been looking for someone else. I have no family except for a sister who never married and my great-nephew, Ian, here, and his parents."

"But perhaps you might know of someone who . . ."

Mr. Li shook his head. "I know few people outside my own family, which, as I said, is very small."

"But years ago?" I persisted. "My dad was in his late forties, so he'd have been born—"

"Years ago, I was a laundryman. From the time we came here in 1932, that is what I was. A laundryman and the owner of laundries. Almost the only people I saw were customers, and all I knew of them was how they liked their shirts to be finished."

A slow *scritch* sounded behind us. A frail, tiny woman dressed in black had turned in, pushing a wheeled walker. I could see a few vegetables in a net bag that hung from one handle. She moved carefully, watching the path, her head bent.

"Ah!" Mr. Li tilted his head toward the sound. "Here is my sister now. Sucheng," he said, "this young woman would like to know if her father, Mr. Steven Chen, came to see us."

The woman looked up then, and I saw her face, pitted and bitterly lined. An emotion that I couldn't read shone briefly in her eyes.

"No," she told me, "there has been no one here. And we do not like to be bothered by strangers."

"Sucheng!" Mr. Li exclaimed.

At that moment a pet flap in the front door squeaked open, and a large gray cat slipped out. It looked at me and then streaked away. Maybe no one at that house, not even Mr. Li with his careful politeness, liked strangers.

I left almost immediately afterward, feeling embarrassed and disappointed and mad at myself for believing I might clear Dad with a short car trip and a few questions.

And thinking about that, I didn't pay close enough attention to driving back more directly than I'd arrived, so that pretty soon I was turned around again.

Then I saw a street name I recognized. Without consciously deciding to do so, I turned and drove past a straggle of small businesses and houses with multiple mailboxes to an intersection that was burned in my mind, though I'd never been there before.

A tire shop with a CLOSED sign stood on one corner, a pawnshop on another. There was a boarded-up gas station and, opposite, the dirty-windowed convenience store where Dad had parked the night he was killed.

I pulled over and sat there for five, maybe ten minutes, trying to imagine and trying not to, and I couldn't have said why I stayed. I hadn't wanted to see where Dad died, and now that I had, it made me angry that the last place he ever saw was this dreary, failed corner.

A patrol car stopped next to me, and the policeman on the passenger side rolled down his window. He nodded toward the map on my dashboard. "Need directions?"

He told me how to get back to the interstate, and the patrol car followed till I'd made the first couple of turns and could see a sign to I-5 in the distance.

I waved a thanks for their help, though sooner or later I'd have found my way without it. It occurred to me, though, that in getting lost twice, I had at least proved to myself how easy it would have been for Dad, if he had gone to see someone in the International District, to have wound up at the convenience store by mistake. Yet since I hadn't established that he had . . .

Caught up in those thoughts, I almost reached the freeway's entrance ramp before I remembered my sweater. I made a U-turn and went back to retrieve it.

By the time I found the Li house, the afternoon sun was slanting at such an angle that blinds were closed all along their side of the street. No one was in the garden, and the pickup truck was gone and also my cardigan.

I went to the door, intending to ring the bell, but querulous voices coming clearly through the thin pet flap stopped me. I heard Mr. Li's sister, Sucheng, say, "You are an old fool, is still what I say. Why did you talk to her?"

He answered, "Because I wished to. How many times are you going to ask?"

"Old fool," she said again. "All these years, and now you put us in danger."

His tone hardened. "I? Are we so old that you forget?" Then, not so hard, "I was only polite. You are upset over nothing."

Footsteps shuffled away, and after a moment I knocked.

"Ah," Mr. Li said to me. "You have come for your wrap. We have brought it inside for safekeeping."

CHAPTER 22

That's one woman I wouldn't want to see again, I thought as I drove home. Although Mr. Li had been gentle. Well, *gentle* wasn't exactly the right word. *Courtly.* A word no one even used anymore, but it fit.

I wondered what old argument I'd stirred up that had made them speak of danger. It was hard to even put them and the idea of danger together. They were too ancient, too frail.

Maybe they were just mixed-up, like the man who'd thought I was from Meals on Wheels. Maybe their minds rearranged people and places and facts.

I shivered. It would be so scary not to be able to count on your mind. If you couldn't trust yourself, who could you trust?

And when it came to scary—that old woman! What was her name? Sucheng? I wondered if she was as mean as she seemed.

I couldn't help being relieved that Mr. Li and his sister didn't seem to be in any way related to Dad. Their world—the sister's anyway—was not one I would want to step into.

But much more, I was discouraged. I'd needed them to be people Dad had visited.

Mom was still out when I got home, and by then I was thinking about the photo again. Maybe the woman in California had remembered the name wrong. Or maybe there was something else written on it that she'd forgotten or hadn't bothered to tell me.

Anyway, I'd thought of a place to look for it.

I went to Mom's bedroom, which was still much the way it had been when Dad shared it. Although Mom had given most of his clothes to the Salvation Army, she'd left on his dresser the items he'd always kept there: a backup alarm clock, a piece of driftwood that looked like a bird in flight, the keepsake box I'd made at camp one summer.

I knew what I'd find inside the box, because Dad had never minded my rummaging through it. There'd be a ribbon I'd won at a fourth grade field day, the pin from a journalism honorary society he'd belonged to, the tag from a Christmas gift from Mom. There'd be odds and ends he'd emptied from his pockets.

And because the box was where he sometimes stashed small items he didn't want to lose, it was where, I thought, he just might have put the photo.

I was right. I found, beneath a hardware store list and a coffee shop punch card, part of a worn and yellowed photograph, with one side and a corner torn raggedly away. It showed a Chinatown street scene, just the way the woman had said.

But when I turned it over, there was enough beyond what she'd told me to make excitement run through me.

Down low, running to the jagged edge, were the words "With best regards." Each letter looked to have been carefully, individually formed.

And under that, the name Li, although it appeared to be a first name. The name that followed it began with an *F* and what might be the start of an *a*. Whatever had followed was missing, gone in the torn-off corner.

And one more word, at the bottom, was partly gone also. But the part that was there had my heart pounding. *Sea*. The first part of *Seattle*.

So Dad *had* known to search here. And the picture on the front would have sent him to the International District, just as Jillian had guessed.

Also—I thought back. Hadn't I learned that the Chinese way was to put the last name first? I was pretty sure. Family name, then given name.

Mr. Li's first name started with an *F*. I'd seen it in the phone book, and he'd said it: "I am Fai-yi Li."

But he'd also said he knew nothing of Dad, and I didn't think he'd lied. There'd been something—I tried to define it. *Honorable*-seeming about him.

I turned the photo to the front side. It showed a couple of cars from the early days of automobiles, followed by a horse-drawn wagon. The people on the crowded street—almost all men—had Chinese faces, and while some wore slope-shouldered wool suits, others wore the work clothes I associated with China of long ago. Signs painted in Chinese characters hung above stores.

But then, looking more closely, I spotted a sign with both Chinese characters and English letters. The tear went through the sign, so that all I could read was HUPIN.

I put Dad's box back on the dresser but kept the picture.

With it, I had something more to go on. But what? *What?*

MIDWIFE, 1936

She came to me in the night, to my home in the back streets of San Francisco. Young and alone. She was apprehensive—as are all who are about to give birth—and afraid, I think, of what lay beyond her when the hours of pain were done and the chore of caring for a baby would be added to the need to provide for herself.

But I saw eagerness in her eyes, too, and gentleness. The baby would be loved.

What I did not see were the wrong things inside her body. If I had, I would not have let her in. A woman such as I, foreign, doing work that officials forbade because I did not have the schooling, the papers—a woman such as I could not have a death on her hands.

But I could not see the things wrong.

The young woman lived such a little while. Long enough to tell me her name. An.

Long enough to tell me she had no family. She had hoped her father might understand her having returned to Seattle to see the baby's father. She had come back here when she failed, but by then it was too late. Her father had already left for China without her.

She lived long enough to extract a promise that I would let the baby's father know he had a daughter.

"Say he might call her Hope," she said. "Here," she added, handing me a picture. "There on the back, you can see his name written. He lives in Seattle and works in the laundry of Dewei Li."

I made the promise in good conscience, to ease her passing, though I knew it was one I would not keep. It might lead to too many questions.

I regretted, though, that the picture got torn and the name mostly lost. But there was so much to do and to think of, and all so quickly, after she died. I only just stopped my neighbor from throwing the picture away entirely.

I doubted that anyone would give much thought to her body when it was found in the alley where he took it for me. Poor people died. It was the way of things.

I carried the infant girl myself to where she would be quickly discovered and cared for. And I tucked the torn picture into the old blanket that I wrapped around her, and I pinned to it a paper with the name her mother had given her, though I had to pay a penny to have it written.

Hope.

Luck *might serve the baby better, I thought. She would need it.*

But naming her baby Hope was the last thing the young woman, An, ever did, except to die. I would not undo it.

CHAPTER 23

In the morning, as early as I could decently call someone on a Sunday, I phoned Jillian. Once I was done apologizing—I could tell from her yawns that I'd woken her up—I said, "You remember the old Seattle photos Lynch had you go through?"

"Yeah. And after all my work, he didn't use any."

"Where were they?"

"They're cataloged online. Or do you mean the originals? Those are at the library. The big one downtown. Why do you want to know?"

"Because I've got an old Chinatown photo that Dad had when he was little. There's a rip right through the only sign that's in English, but if I could find a scene like it, maybe I could read the rest. It might not mean anything, of course."

"But it's all you've got, right?"

"Right."

"So I'll meet you at the library after lunch. I think it's open Sunday afternoons."

A man at the Central Library's information desk sent us to the hushed Seattle Room, a soaring space with a balcony overlooking the general reading area. It seemed special even in a building as spectacular as the library itself, with its swooping glass walls and rising lines of books that invited you up and up. I paused at the room's entrance, uncertain.

"Whoa! Pretty fancy!" Jillian said.

A woman wearing a library badge joined us. "Beautiful, isn't it? You're welcome to come in and look around. Or are you girls here for something in particular?"

I handed her the torn photo. "It's got the start of *Seattle* written on the back, so I'm hoping it was taken here," I said. "I was wondering if the library might have another photograph of the same street. One that would show the rest of that sign that's partly in English."

"It looks like a professional shot," the librarian said. Turning it over, she pointed to faint marks on the back, so faded I hadn't noticed them. "A postcard, maybe? The stock's heavy enough. And we do have historical postcards. You might go through those, on the chance you'll find a match."

She brought out two long boxes, but before she let us get into them, she asked if we'd ever handled archival materials. When we said we hadn't, she gave us throwaway cotton gloves and put on a pair herself.

"Even with these, you need to be careful not to touch the images," she said. "Handle the postcards by the edges. Don't set anything down on them. One card out at a time, and keep them in order."

At first, cowed by the white gloves and warnings, we worked slowly, pulling out and putting back waterfront scenes and pictures of Pike Place Market as it used to be.

Then, as we got the feel of the work, we sped up. And Jillian, of course, started talking.

"So, did you used to read *Nancy Drew*s?" she asked. "Because this is kind of like you're Nancy and I'm George. Or maybe Bess. No, George, I think, although of course I don't look like her. I mean, didn't she always keep her hair short? And I don't remember curls. But you're Nancy, definitely, even if I'm closer to blond than you. It's a style thing, and . . ."

Despite her chatter, Jillian worked efficiently, barely glancing at postcards that clearly weren't a match, pausing occasionally to compare a street scene with the picture I'd brought.

And for a while I made good progress, too. I slowed down, though, once I discovered that many of the cards had actually been written and mailed. Reading them was like riding a train at night, catching brief glimpses into lighted rooms where people you don't know are eating or washing dishes, watching television, arguing.

"Will be out for the new baby . . ."

"The teacherage is drafty and the size of a closet, but it's better than rooming about . . ."

Dad, I thought, would have been fascinated.

"More salmon to eat than you ever did see . . ."

"Aiming to walk around Mt. Rainier. Can you imagine?"

I got so involved that I was startled when the librarian came over to ask how we were coming along.

"I'm coming along fine," Jillian said. "My friend's bogged down."

The librarian laughed. "We probably ought to put up a warning sign: CAUTION—DANGER ZONE FOR INQUISITIVE MINDS."

回

We reached the end of the postcards without having found even a partial match, and I went back to my original idea of going through the library's collection of historical photos.

"Grab a couple of computers and get comfortable," the librarian said. "We've got more than thirty thousand images. And hang on to the gloves, in case you want to see an actual print."

I was even slower going through the cataloged photographs than I'd been with the postcards, but now the problem was with the pictures themselves. Many of them showed Chinatown streets lined with shops that were confusingly similar, with signs that were hard to make out, and I had just that one fragment of an English word to look for.

Jillian even stopped talking so she could concentrate, and for a couple of hours we worked in such quiet that her sudden "Got it!" made me jump about a mile.

"I think I do, anyway," she added.

The picture on her screen had been taken from a different angle, but most of the shops were the same as those in my photo. And the building she was pointing to had the same brick cornices and the same heavy woodwork around the windows.

She zoomed in on a sign, but it was too fuzzy to read.

The librarian, who'd come over at Jillian's "Got it!" said she'd get the original.

It was beautiful, an eight-by-ten-inch black-and-white enlargement, crystal sharp and full of detail.

The sign, examined with a magnifying glass, was clear. The part in English said HUPING HUANG, HERBALIST, the words stacked one atop another.

I wrote it down and then asked the librarian, "If I wanted to find out about Huping Huang, how could I do it?"

"You might check our genealogy collection, although it's so near to closing time you'd need to come back another day."

She pursed her lips. "Or you might want to begin at NARA—the National Archives and Records Administration. Its regional depository is near the university."

"What would be there?" I asked.

"Immigration records."

When Jillian suggested going for food before leaving downtown, I told her my mom was expecting me home for dinner. I said I had time for a soda, though.

As we walked, looking for a place that was open, she asked, "When will you try that National Archives place? Since it's government, it probably shuts down right at five p.m, and you're not off again till Friday."

"I'm going tomorrow," I told her. "I think Fran will let me take some time, and if not, I guess I'll take it anyway."

Jillian gave me a quick look. "That doesn't sound like you."

"It's not," I said. "But with all that's happening, or that could happen, Friday's just too far away to follow up on the only idea I've got for clearing Dad."

"Okay, then," she said, sounding both amused and impressed. "Go, Maggie!" She pointed to a café across the street. "How about there?"

We took our drinks—and her soup and salad special—to a window table. "I'll eat fast so you won't be late getting home," she said. "I guess your mom's pretty different from mine. Regular meals and all."

"They're not as regular as when Dad was around to insist we got our family time in," I told her.

Laughing, Jillian said, "I can't imagine it. My father, even when he *was* around, never grasped the concept of family." She said it as matter-of-factly as if she'd been commenting on the soup.

"So," she went on, "I guess your dad was pretty good, as fathers go?"

"He was great," I said.

"And what was the best thing about him?"

Surprised, I tried to read her expression. I saw only interest.

"No one's ever asked me that," I said. "Mainly, people talk about what a good journalist he was." I pleated a paper napkin while I thought. "But I guess the best thing—from my view—was that he had a lot of faith in me."

"And what else was good?" she asked.

"He never talked down to me. When I got interested in something, it became important to him. And he and Mom, together, were always coming up with great adventures, like . . ."

And then, because she was too busy eating to keep up her side of the conversation, I went on to tell her about that first ocean birthday. About how Dad had helped me understand that there were lands and people way beyond the horizon.

And that it was a *beyond* that you could go to, if you wanted. If you dared.

I got to the end of the story before I realized what she'd done. Just as Jake had waited, interviewing the Mariners, Jillian had waited out my first answers so that I would give her a better one.

All she said, though, was, "Nice. He must have loved you and your mother a lot."

"Yes," I said. "He did."

CHAPTER 24

"Are you sick?" Fran asked the next morning when I called for permission to go in late.

"No. I've got a personal matter to take care of. About Dad."

"Maggie," she said, "you can't—"

"It's not anything that would cause problems for the paper. I promise."

I knew she wanted to ask for details, but she didn't. "Go ahead, then," she said finally. "Take the morning. You can make it up Friday."

I angled over to the Sandpoint Way NE address I'd found for the National Archives Pacific Alaska Region. A concrete sign with its name sat behind a small flower garden, and more flowers surrounded the entrance to a solid-looking white building.

I told the man working at the reception desk that I was trying to pick up a family search my father had started.

"Genealogy's a catching bug!" he said. "Though usually the people who've caught it aren't quite so young."

"The only thing I have to go on is a Chinese name from a long time ago."

"Let me get you set up," he said, "and then I'll turn you over to an archivist who's an expert in that area."

I showed him my driver's license, and he logged me in and gave me a researcher's card. "No packs or bags of any kind in the reading area. No pens, either. Pencils only, or did you bring a computer?"

"No."

"Then pencil and paper. All right, let's go."

The archivist was a friendly, vivacious woman who was excited about my interest in Chinese immigration. "If you'd like a tour, I'll show you what we have," she said. "People have no idea!"

She led me into a long section of floor-to-ceiling shelves filled with vertical document boxes. "These are all Chinese immigration and legal records. A treasure trove for researchers."

Explaining about wanting to track down the person my dad might have visited recently in searching for his family, I showed her Huping Huang's name. "He must be dead by now, but I'd like to know if his family—his descendents—might still be living in Seattle."

"You're not going to learn that here," she said. "But there might be something in his file that would point you in the right direction."

"And you'd have a file on him?"

"We might, if he was a naturalized citizen or alien worker, and if he came through the Port of Seattle. Do you know what year he would have immigrated here?"

"I don't know that he did," I said.

"Or when he might have left to visit or move back to China?"

"I really don't know anything about him at all except that he was an herbalist," I admitted. "I got his name from an old photograph. Can't we just look it up?"

"I wish it was as simple as checking an alphabetical list, but it's not," the archivist said. "Even where we have lists, names can be a problem because of inconsistencies in how immigration officials interpreted and spelled what they heard."

"And no one corrected them?" I asked.

"Identification papers specifying an immigrant's right to be in the United States were so precious and often so hard to obtain, I doubt that many would have risked quarreling with anything on them. Probably they just accepted their new names. Anyway, usually the easiest way to get into a record is via an entry or sailing date."

Discouraged, I said, "I don't know any dates at all, except for 1932, when a Fai-yi Li, or Li Fai-yi, came here with his sister. But that doesn't help, because even though I first thought he might be related, apparently he's not."

"If it's even a possibility, and assuming we have a file on him, you might want to look through it anyway," she said. "It might contain references to other family members or connections."

"And I'd be allowed to?"

"A 1932 file should be open. Generally, to protect privacy, we apply the seventy-five-year rule in determining what's available to the public."

Soon I was settled at a table in the researchers' work area, reading pages pinned in a manila folder for LI, FAI-YI.

The top sheet was a long form with information inked in and a photograph attached. The boy pictured looked solemn and scared and way too young to bear any resemblance to the old Mr. Li I'd met.

Reading down the form, I learned that Fai-yi Li was fifteen years old when he arrived in this country. He was five feet eight inches tall, and he weighed 139 pounds. Identification marks included a mole on his neck.

At the bottom of the page was the notation "S/N."

I searched out the archivist who'd helped me and asked her what the *S/N* meant.

"Son of native," she answered. "*Native* was the term usually used for an ethnic Chinese born on American soil."

The multi-page transcript of an interrogation followed the form sheet, with questions so random I couldn't imagine why they'd been asked.

The young man's answers told how many steps there were to the front door of his home in China. How many rooms were in the house and how many children lived there, where the school was and the village well.

The archivist paused by my chair. "Finding anything helpful?"

"Not so far. I'm reading the things he was asked when he arrived here, but the questions are weird. Why would anybody care about the details of his Chinese village?"

"Because someone only pretending to be from there might not have been able to answer the questions," she said. "Or he might have tried but gotten tripped up telling inconsistent lies. The interrogations were designed to uncover deceit."

"But why would—"

"It was the Exclusion Era," she said. "It began once Chinese labor was no longer needed to help open up the West—by building railroads, primarily. For the next sixty years or so, until the middle of World War II, federal laws severely restricted immigration. Generally, unless they came in under one of a few special classifications—students, for instance—or unless they were already American citizens because one of their parents was, ethnic Chinese didn't get in."

"So people tried to get around the laws?" I asked.

Nodding, she said, "It was often quite sad. Some paid to have themselves smuggled in, risking their lives in horrible ways. Some who had come here in the early years took advantage of the 1906 San Francisco earthquake to gain citizenship, saying that records of their birth were among those that burned.

"And," she continued, "still others sought entry here by falsely claiming to be the children of American citizens. Such 'paper son' schemes required connivance at this end— someone, usually but not always a relative, willing to claim them and able to provide a convincing story.

"Efforts to discover paper sons included interrogations like the one you're looking at. A single inconsistent answer could cause a hopeful immigrant to be declared illegal."

"And then, if he was?" I asked.

"He'd be sent back. And immigration officials might take a new interest in the status of the supposed parent, too."

No wonder the kid in the photograph looked scared, I thought.

I remembered the angry snatch of words I'd overheard Mr. Li and his sister exchange—"All these years, and now you put us in danger." Maybe this explained what I had heard. Maybe they'd come here as part of a paper son scheme. Would anyone care about that after all this time?

I returned to my reading, finding more of the same questions repeated over and over in different ways. And then they took a new tack. The questioner said, "We've a report of a crime that you were involved in before you left China. What do you know about that?"

"What crime?" Li asked.

"A crime. You tell us."

Now, as the questions and answers went back and forth, the interrogator became increasingly accusing. "It was reported . . . It was reported."

Li repeated, "I do not know. I do not know."

And then suddenly the questioner said, "Enough. You're believed."

There was little more after that. That was the end of the transcript.

"What happened?" I asked the archivist, who was reading over my shoulder. "Why the sudden decision?"

"Probably he convinced them," she said.

"But what were those questions about a crime all about?"

"Who knows? They might have been trying to correlate his story with things they'd heard from other immigrants. Or the questions might have been a setup for demanding a bribe. There are certainly accounts of corrupt immigration officials and translators among the good ones. But," she went on, "we've gotten sidetracked. Look what I've found for you."

For the first time, I saw that she'd brought over a much smaller file. "This might be your herbalist," she said. "Same name spelling and the right occupation."

CHAPTER 25

There were only a couple of pages. The first was an application made by Huping Huang, a Chinese merchant living in the United States, for a permit to be allowed to reenter this country following a proposed visit to China with his daughter, An Huang, who was an American citizen.

The reentry permit was granted, but it appeared never to have been used, since the file's last notation was just a ship name and the date of its departure from San Francisco in 1935.

So, I thought, *apparently he left this country and never came back.*

I looked for anything on the form that might help me. His marital status was listed as widower; the daughter was his only child.

"Would there be a file on the daughter?" I asked.

The archivist clicked her tongue as she considered. "As an American citizen—no. As an ethnic Chinese—possibly. It wouldn't hurt to look."

A few minutes later she handed me one last file, and giving me an odd look, she said, "I'll leave you to go through this one by yourself."

I opened it and looked at a picture of a teenage girl.

Of course, the girl's old-fashioned clothes and blunt haircut were unfamiliar, but her face . . . It was the face I saw when I looked in a mirror. Or so similar to it, anyway, that I felt blood rushing through me and my heart beating fast. Goose bumps raised on my arms, and my breath came shallow.

This girl was *me,* except she was so much lovelier. A girl who looked more gentle than I could ever be. But perhaps she was defiant, too? Somehow she seemed to be both.

And sad. She looked very, very sad.

I could feel the archivist discreetly watching from across the room, and I made myself read.

There wasn't much in the file. Even less information than in her father's—just an approved request for a reentry permit and, later, a brief notation from an official who had checked to see if she ever actually left the United States. Dated in 1936, the entry ended, "Deceased, San Francisco."

I left the archives with a photocopy of An's picture. I hadn't asked for it. The archivist just gave it to me, along with a look that said she understood that I couldn't trust myself to talk just then.

I went only a few blocks, though, before realizing that it wasn't safe for me to drive. The tears filling my eyes made traffic a blur, and when I switched lanes, I saw a car appear from nowhere on my left. After that, I pulled into the first parking lot I came to and stopped the car at the deserted far end.

Hugging the steering wheel, I waited out waves of emotion. I felt as though all the adrenaline my body was capable of producing was pumping through me, and that if I didn't hang on to the wheel, I might explode through my skin.

I was beyond keyed up. I was excited and frightened and also . . .

I picked up the picture. Also, I felt robbed.

Looking at An made me furious because it was as though the fact of her meant I wasn't the first person in the world who was me.

Which I knew was crazy. Even crazier was that I kept looking at her picture, when all I had to do was turn my gaze away.

Suddenly I remembered another of those ocean birthdays. I was older, allowed beyond the breaker line for the first time. A particularly big wave had risen from the rolling swell, and Dad had shouted that it was one to dive into. But I couldn't stop watching it, even when he'd shouted, "Now, Maggie! *Now!*"

I'd watched, eyes wide open, until the moment it crashed down and pummeled me, flailing and choking, through the plunging surf.

"It was your fault," I'd yelled at Dad. "You shouldn't have let me go out there. It's your fault I got hurt." And I'd cried the way I wanted to cry now, because I remembered how that breaker had hurt and because I didn't want to see this picture that I couldn't stop looking at.

It wasn't fair that this was what I'd found. I'd gone to the archives for Dad's sake, hoping to pick up a trace of his steps.

And yes, I'd thought I wanted to know who his real family was. Who mine was. I'd thought replacing the part that had gone missing would help me feel like my old, familiar self again.

Instead my search had taken me to a terrifying world I didn't want to know about. It had shown me teenagers who gave up their true identities for the rest of their lives.

It had tied me to a girl who died when she wasn't much older than I, leaving a photo that said she had a story that was big and sad.

My thoughts were all tangled up, and I felt sick and outraged for her, too.

"Why? How?" I said aloud, as though the girl's picture might answer.

And then I did start crying, and I cried and I cried.

I cried because I'd failed Dad. Because I'd run out of ideas for how I might find out about the day he died.

I cried for that scared kid, Fai-yi Li, in that long-ago interrogation room.

I cried for An, the girl who was and wasn't me and who surely was my ancestor.

And I cried for the unknown person between us. There must have been someone besides Dad . . . before him.

HOPE JOYCE CHEN 2009

Where do seventy plus years of a life go?

Is there a set portion for regret?

And if so, which parts of my portion would I replace with ones less haunting? Which parts of my life would I change?

Perhaps it would be my regret, when I watched the older girls leave Chinatown, that I was not old enough to go with them. The war had brought money to their parents and uniforms to their brothers, and it had opened office doors for them.

I followed not too many years later.

Perhaps, instead, I should have stayed with the old couple who had treated me like a daughter, giving me their name and trying to raise me as they had been raised.

Perhaps I would have stayed if they had not been so honest, if they had not told me someone else had first called me Hope, *and if they had not also given me two things that they themselves had not purchased. A ragged blanket that I eventually lost. A torn postcard I took with me when I ran away.*

Or perhaps my real regrets began a few years later, when I'd saved enough to pay my way into a secretarial school. For if I hadn't gone there, hadn't graduated and found a position, hadn't fallen in love where I shouldn't . . .

Well. At least I have no regrets for the infant. However his life has turned out, surely it has been better than any I could have provided.

And although I never saw him after the day he was born, I did give him as much as I was given. More.

There were papers to complete, and even though I knew it would prob-

ably be changed, I gave him a name: Steven Chen. And when I handed the signed forms back to the agency lady, I gave her the beautiful, soft blanket that was the most expensive thing I had ever bought. "This is for him," I said, "and also this old postcard."

She examined it, puzzled. "Why is it important?"

"I don't know," I answered. "But when I was a baby, someone left it with me."

So again I ask, where have the years gone?

My twenty-five became thirty-five. A decade became two and then three and four. I reached the end of working. Another decade went by.

I'm well past seventy now. With what? Another ten, twenty more years in front of me? I can live them as I've lived thus far, on my own.

Except, lately I've thought . . .

Perhaps it's just seeing my women friends move away from San Francisco to be nearer to sons and daughters. But I've started thinking that one day, even though I still live in this city where I was born, I'll be alone in a land of strangers.

I know there are places where missing people can leave their names. Registries for parents who want to find children. For children who want to find parents.

I wish I could know whether, if I were to leave my name, it would become a regret.

CHAPTER 26

The early afternoon hum was already picking up when I got to the newsroom. In Lifestyles, Deena handed me a new batch of contest entries, but I'd barely started opening them when Jillian came over, bringing two mugs of tea.

"I'm working with Lynch again," she said, "but I told him I needed a break. How did it go this morning? Did you track down the name we got off the sign?"

"Huping Huang," I said. "Yes. I saw files on him and his daughter, but there wasn't anything in them about anyone who'd be alive today."

That was all I meant to say, but I couldn't keep the rest of it in.

"They were my family, though. I saw her photograph, and she looked just like me. And I read that she died not long after the picture was taken."

"No wonder you came in looking like you needed tea," Jillian said. "I once heard about this person who, you know, could get in touch with her earlier lives, and—"

She broke off. "I'm sorry. That must have been hard. And you must be really disappointed you didn't learn anything to help your father."

Jillian came back in midafternoon, just after I finished the recipes.

"I've got an idea," she said. "That shop—Huang's—was in Seattle's Chinatown. Probably he and his daughter lived nearby, because people did live close to their work in those days, and as Chinese, the Huangs probably weren't welcome many other places." She shot me a quick look. "I don't mean that wrong," she said. "But things were different back then."

"I know that," I said. "What are you getting at?"

"That for those same reasons, Mr. Li—" She paused. "That's the name of the old man you talked to, right? The one who still lives in the area?"

I nodded. I'd told her about him while we were working at the library.

"So my idea is that there couldn't have been that many teenagers in Chinatown when he was a kid. They probably at least knew each other. So I think you should ask Mr. Li if he remembers Mr. Huang's daughter, and if he knows if any of her family still lives in the area. Because if they do, and your father had found that out, then—"

I stopped her. "I can't go back there," I said.

"Why not?"

"Because I can't." To my horror, I felt the tears well up again. "Because I don't *want* to."

"I don't understand," Jillian said.

I looked down, trying to think how I could explain a truth that I was ashamed of.

Finally I said, "Do you remember our first day here, how you took me for an ethnic pick?"

"One of my better blunders, huh?" Jillian said with a little laugh. "And you gave me a look that froze me out."

"That's because that's not how I think of myself. I have a heritage, sure—everyone has that, and I'm proud of mine. But it doesn't make me foreign, and it doesn't mean I have to take on the problems of a bunch of people I don't understand."

Jillian waited, her face difficult to read.

I said, "I don't want to change who I am, even if sometimes I'm not sure who that is."

Jillian still didn't respond.

I tried again, hearing a plea creep into my voice and feeling my face go hot. "Seeing An Huang's picture, knowing we have to be related, made me realize that if I keep up this hunt, I might find a family I don't want. And then, even if I never see them again, I'll know about them, and that will make me different."

I groped for a better way to explain. "It's like when somebody dies. Nothing changes for you unless you know."

"So?" Jillian finally said.

"So," I said, "I don't want to see Mr. Li or his sister again, because I don't want to know more about An Huang."

Jillian took a moment to think about that. Then, "Got it," she said. "You'd rather leave your dad to whatever stories people make up about him than take a chance on finding a truth you might not like. That's cool."

I felt like I'd been slapped. "You don't mean that."

She got up. "No, I don't. If I had a father who came anywhere close to being as great as you say yours was, I'd do everything I could to take care of him."

“Look,” I said. “Wait. It’s not as though it’s very likely that Mr. Li would know anybody who—”

“You’re right,” she said. “The possibility that you might learn anything useful from him is probably so remote it’s not worth upsetting yourself over. But I’m glad I brought it up, because now we’re even.”

“What do you mean?”

“We’ve each had to let go of some ideas. You were wrong about me, thinking I didn’t have a brain in my head, right up till you read my writing. And I was wrong, right up till now, thinking I’d like to be like you.”

Fran wasn’t around to ask if I could leave early, so I asked Deena, who seemed relieved not to have to find another task to keep me busy.

On my way out of the newsroom I detoured by Photo. Jillian was working at a computer monitor that displayed several almost-identical pictures of kids playing under a lawn sprinkler.

“I see what you meant about changing the depth of field,” she said, turning. Then, “Oh! I thought you were Lynch.”

“About our talk. I just wanted to let you know I heard what you said. I’m going out there now.”

CHAPTER 27

Mr. Li's sister answered their door. "Now is not good for a visit," she said.

But he'd come to the door also, and he invited me into their small living room, where a chess game was in progress. "You remember my nephew, Ian? You have come at a fine time. He was about to say *checkmate.*"

Mr. Li reached across the board, his fingers brushing the outlines of pieces until he found Ian's white queen. He moved her diagonally, tipped over his own black king, and said, "There, nephew. I have saved you having to embarrass me."

They both laughed easily, although Sucheng Li, looking on, did not join in.

"Please," Mr. Li said to me, "do sit down. I heard you tell my sister you have thought of another question for us. Are you still searching for the people your father might have come to see in this neighborhood?"

"I think I may have found the family," I said.

I was interrupted by my cell phone, its ringtone jarring in that setting. Apologizing, I ended the call without looking to see who it was from, switched the phone to silent, and laid it on the table.

"The reason I've come back," I said, "is that the names I have are from a long time ago, from about when you came over from China. I know the people are no longer here, but I hope you might remember them and know of any relatives or descendents."

"And their names?" Mr. Li asked.

"Huping Huang and his daughter, An. He was an herbalist, and she—"

I broke off, stopped by Mr. Li's sudden stillness, so complete it seemed unnatural.

"Are you all right?" I asked.

He brought himself to with a small jerk. "I do remember them," he said, "but I know nothing that can help you."

His manner had become even more formal, as though he was being careful not to say too much.

I thought of my guess that he and his sister had come to this country illegally. Perhaps he was reluctant to talk about any part of that time.

"Please," I said, "I won't cause you trouble. I just need to find somebody who can say why my father was in this area the day he was killed. Otherwise he may always be suspected of doing something really wrong."

"I do not understand," Mr. Li said.

"My father was a journalist, and the police think he may have taken money for hushing up a crime he'd learned about. They think that might be why he came here. But Dad wasn't like that. I'm sure the only dishonest thing he ever did was make up a story about where he'd come from, and he only kept that going because he loved my mother and me."

Mr. Li closed his eyes briefly before saying, "I would help you if I could, Miss Chen. But I know nothing of your father. Sucheng, do you?"

"No." Her hand pushed on my shoulder. "You go now."

I'd known, of course, that Mr. Li and his sister weren't likely to be able to help me. That's what I'd told Jillian. But now I realized how much I was counting on them to have some answers, anyway. And I was surprised at how let down I felt.

As I stood, I made one last try. Taking the copy of An's picture from my bag, I said to Sucheng Li, "Would you please just look at this picture of An Huang? Maybe then you might remember something."

She barely glanced at it. "No," she said.

But Ian, who'd stood up with me, was staring first at it and then at me. "She looks just like you!" he exclaimed. And then, "Auntie! Look again!"

"I saw. It means nothing." Sucheng Li gave me a little shove. "Now you leave!"

"No!" Mr. Li said. His voice strained, he asked, "Nephew, is what you say true?"

"Absolutely," Ian answered. "It's like they could be the same person."

Mr. Li turned away then, but I could still see his profile and the emotions playing across his face. I saw him go from uncertain to sad, to angry, and then to . . . A word came to mind that I knew but had never used: *implacable.*

"And you said it means nothing? What else have you lied about, Sucheng?" he asked quietly. "Perhaps about Miss Chen's father? Was he here after all?"

Then it was his sister's face that emotions raced across, stretching and deepening its pitted crevasses.

She cackled suddenly. "Yes, and I sent him away. Sent him and sent her. I told her to have her brat on the street, and you never knew. You never knew anything I didn't want you to. Did you?"

She laughed again, an ugly laugh like a crow's cry. "Did you?"

Ian, appearing bewildered, asked, "Who?" He turned to me. "Did you come here another time and see my aunt? Are you—?"

But Mr. Li understood that his sister wasn't talking about me.

"An?" he asked. "An came to us for help and you sent her away? And she was with child? When?"

A smile curved Sucheng Li's mouth. "When do you think? While you were off running after her. You should not have left me. I told you that then."

Another call made my cell phone flash. I quickly stopped it.

"Who is An?" Ian asked.

Mr. Li answered, "An was my . . . I thought at one time that she was my wife."

He stopped then and didn't continue until I finally said, "But she wasn't?"

"I was told she was not," he said. "That our marriage was illegal and that I would not see her again. Even so, I looked for her. But when I heard her father had taken her to China, then I knew—" He frowned and corrected himself. "Then I *believed* that she was gone forever. I have always believed it, until now."

"Fool, you!" said his sister, and making a spitting sound, she left the room.

She could just as well not have been in the house, for all the attention Mr. Li and Ian gave her departure.

"I had thought never to tell this," Mr. Li said to Ian. "I had thought that all the harm that could be done already had been done, long ago." He turned to me. "It seems I was wrong about that, also."

"I don't get it," Ian said. "I'm sorry about what happened to you and that girl, An, but it *was* so long ago. How can that hurt anyone now?"

Mr. Li sighed. "There are incorrect things that you have believed about me," he said. "About what I am to you and your father. Or, I should say, about what I am not."

For a moment he appeared to drift into some private byway of thoughts. Then, with a small flutter of his hands, he said, "But you have a right to know. And Miss Chen?"

"Yes?" I said.

"I think perhaps you have even more of a right. I think it will explain what brought your father to this house and why my sister lied about that."

Once more my phone flashed. The screen said, "Call me now! J."

Another message flashed. "NOW!"

Apologizing to Mr. Li, I said, "I keep getting urgent telephone messages from work. Do you mind if I—"

"Please," he said. "What I have to say has waited many years. Make your call, and then we will talk."

Jillian answered at once. "It's about time!" she said. "And after the hassle I had digging up a cell number for you. You really ought to—"

"Jillian!" I said. "What?"

"Oh! I called to say that you can stop. Getting involved, I

mean. Harrison just now came in with Gary Maitlen, all excited, and they got Fran, and I just had a feeling it was about the Galinger story and all, so I followed them right to Mr. Braden's office and—"

"Please," I said. "Just tell me!"

"I am. I told them that if that *was* what they were working on, and if they'd learned something about your dad, then it was only fair—"

"Now!"

"Okay! If you don't want context. The news person who got paid off? It was a woman from a TV station, and she's turned herself in. She got scared that if she didn't come forward and admit to taking money, the police might think she was into even more of the bad stuff."

"So . . . ?" I said, needing Jillian to spell it out, afraid I'd understood wrong.

"So everyone knows it wasn't your dad who Yeager paid off."

I disconnected, feeling as though all the air had been knocked from me. Dad was okay. His name had been cleared without my help, and now it didn't matter what had brought him to the International District the day he was killed.

Relief flooded through me as I also realized I didn't need to learn more about Mr. Li or An Huang, either. Didn't need to take them any further into my life.

"That was the newspaper," I told Mr. Li. "The authorities have the journalist who was taking bribes, so now everyone knows it wasn't my father. It's no longer important why Dad came to this part of town."

With a glance at Ian, who looked braced for something he didn't want to hear, I added, "I'm really sorry for the trouble I've caused. I'll go now."

"Of course. If that is what you wish," Mr. Li said.

But he made it a question, and he waited.

He was giving me a choice. I could stay to hear, for a different reason now, what he had to say, or I could decide not to.

I knew what I wanted to do.

I wanted to go out the door and go back to being the daughter of the Steven Chen I'd known growing up—no more than that, and no less. Except for Mom, no one other than the people in this house knew that the past he had claimed was a lie, and she wanted to forget.

And of course Jillian knew, but she, I thought, would keep my secret.

I could do it—could leave—as easily as I'd torn up the notebook page where Dad had written "Progress on family project, finally?"

Or this time I could choose to look beyond, to the truths of people I knew and people I didn't. It was what Dad would have expected of his daughter and the way I would like to think of myself.

And so, though I felt scared, I sat down. "I think," I told Mr. Li, "I'd like to stay."

No one said anything for several moments while Mr. Li seemed to be gathering his thoughts.

Then, "You must understand," he began, "this story starts not here but across the ocean, in the place where Sucheng and I were born."

CHAPTER 28

Mom called, "Maggie! Haven't you left yet? I think we need more chips."

"I'm going. I'll pick some up."

It was a Saturday, a few weeks after that late afternoon when the pieces of who I was had rearranged themselves. Mom was in a company's-coming tizzy, even though we'd already cleaned the house, set the table, and gotten most of the cooking done.

We wouldn't put the salmon on the grill until Mr. Li and Ian and Ian's parents arrived.

That wouldn't be for several more hours, and meanwhile I'd promised Jillian to meet her at the mall. We planned to buy new swimsuits for our trip to the San Juans the next day. We were going to catch the first ferry, so that by midmorning we'd be with Bett and Aimee. I hoped my friends would like one another. I thought they would.

Actually, a couple of things Jillian had said made me think they'd all already gotten in touch with one another and that they were conniving to run a line of potential boyfriends by me. Which was okay. I was ready to try a new one.

"And maybe get crackers and a wedge of cheese," Mom called.

"I'm on it."

As I drove, I thought how impossible it seemed that just a couple of months earlier, I hadn't known Mr. Li or Jillian.

Hadn't even been inside the *Herald,* and now I felt at home there and knew that I belonged.

I was still learning the work, of course. Still making mistakes. Still shifting from job to job, helping out where I was needed. Jake had asked for me back on Sports. Fran had me doing rewrites. Harrison occasionally took me out on assignments.

He was still tracking the Galinger story, but there probably weren't any surprises left. Of the people who had been involved in the crime, only J. A. Garcia remained unaccounted for. One theory was that he was an undocumented worker who'd slipped back into the shadow world of illegals.

Ralph Galinger was in jail, having been picked up at the Los Angeles airport trying to catch an overseas flight. He was charged with deliberate homicide, and the corruption story that had emerged from his mostly unsuccessful plea-bargaining was pretty much exactly as we'd figured, right up to the murder part, which we hadn't foreseen.

Or perhaps Harrison and the others had recognized that possibility, too, and it was another reason they'd taken me off the story.

Anyway, the Galinger-Yeager scheme had started to unravel when the TV reporter stumbled onto it and demanded money for keeping it to herself. Tobias Yeager had paid, but he told Donald Landin about it.

And then, after Yeager's death, Landin had appropriated the blackmailing idea, threatening Galinger with giving the whole story to the *Herald.*

"But why did he call you to actually arrange a meeting?" I asked when Harrison was explaining it.

"Maybe he thought Galinger might try to find out if the

threat was real. Or maybe Landin had some cockeyed idea that if Galinger didn't come through with money to keep him quiet, the *Herald* would pay him to talk."

"Stupid," I said.

"Yeah, and suicidal," Harrison agreed.

Because Galinger, an expert marksman in his army days, had gone to where Landin lived and shot him in front of his apartment.

But then, as Galinger was leaving the area, he saw my father, recognizing him from business meetings Dad had covered. And he panicked, afraid Landin had already talked. That time the weapon Galinger aimed was his car.

I could hardly bear to think about it.

But I was very glad I'd had a part in bringing him to justice.

And glad, too, that because of the story Harrison and I found, the Eastside town that was at the center of it had begun inching toward positive change.

Its mayor, though, remained angry with the *Herald* over the bad publicity. Former Galinger Construction employees were now looking for jobs. And people who'd had building projects under way with Galinger Construction were wondering how the work was going to get finished.

"So our story mattered, but it wasn't good for everyone," I said.

"No," Harrison agreed. "News often is a mixed bag, just like the truth can be. All we can do is report what we know and have faith that in the long run, our readers will be better off for being informed."

Seeing the mall entrance ahead, I refocused my attention on parking and finding Jillian.

She was already in the store where we'd agreed to meet, and she already had her arms full of swimsuits for us to try on. They involved every color of the rainbow.

Later on, Mom raised her eyebrows when I showed her the one I picked out. There wasn't time to discuss it, because our dinner guests were pulling into the driveway.

I ran out to meet them. This was the first time they'd come to our home, though I'd often been back to Mr. Li's.

Actually, recently I'd begun to call him Grandfather Li. I'd thought that would be hard, but it had turned out to feel good. *Great-grandfather Li* seemed too much to say, although we were both sure that's what he was to me.

Maybe one day we'd have proof. With Mom's permission, we'd begun contacting agencies that might have information about Dad's birth parents. All we needed to find was the one missing generation. And since he was never adopted, we were hopeful that his name might lead us to his father and mother.

Meanwhile, Mr. Li, Mom and me, and Ian and his folks were all readjusting our notions of family.

It had been hardest on Ian, I thought, finding out that his beloved great-uncle wasn't a real relative. Not by blood.

But the last time I went over, they had the chessboard out again and were saying "Uncle watch your pawn," and "Nephew, your move."

Mr. Li's paper son status—and Sucheng Li's, as a paper

daughter—were legal matters out in the open now. Mr. Li, accompanied by Ian's dad, who was a lawyer, had gone to Immigration Services and given their real names.

No one was certain what the outcome would be, but I wasn't too worried. I couldn't believe anyone would spend time pursuing an illegal entry made more than seventy-five years ago by a man now so elderly.

And I was sure no one would go after Sucheng Li, who lived in her own shadow world of madness.

Our dinner party was a success, and after our guests left, Mom and I sank gratefully into chairs to talk it over.

We were talking a lot these days. And we were remembering and bringing Dad back into our lives, where he'd gone missing.

Sometimes we speculated about how and when he began trying to be someone he wasn't. I thought perhaps he had started by deceiving himself, when being a lonely heart had got to be too hard.

Mom thought his complicated lie might have started by accident. "That first time I brought him home to meet my parents, he mentioned a summer job he'd had in the public relations office of a Boston museum. They knew the museum because its Thomas and Adele Chen Memorial Fund had supported some of their research. I think they may have just jumped to the conclusion that was his family."

"Did he tell them it wasn't?" I asked.

"Maybe he tried. I don't know if they gave him a chance."

"But he never tried to tell you the truth?"

"Maybe, early on," she said. "I might not have given him a chance, either. Or maybe he did tell me, but using words I wouldn't hear."

Now, sitting there with Mom, that's what I kept returning to. Even if we could somehow have Dad back and ask him what happened, he might not have a black-and-white answer to give. More likely, even for him, the answer would be in shades of gray.

But even though I realized that, I also knew it had been Dad's choice to live with his lies. Just as, finally, I believed, Dad had chosen to find the truth about who Steven Chen really was.

It would have been a choice not all that different, I thought, from the one I made when I stayed to hear Mr. Li's story, the part beyond what I already knew, whatever it might mean for me.

A FINAL WORD

I promised to tell you what I know about Fai-yi Li, and I have done that, though perhaps you know more. Perhaps you have heard his voice, perhaps been brushed by other whispers, too.

I also promised to tell you about myself. And although I have done so truthfully, I think I began with a statement that was only partly right. I said the important thing to know about me is that I am Steven's Chen's daughter.

I am, of course. His and Mom's.

But the important thing to know is that I'm more than that.

I think I understand what Dad meant, saying that at sixteen I don't need to decide who I want to be for the rest of my life.

I think that if he could have had just a few more minutes to talk—if he hadn't already stayed too long when he had a plane to catch and Seattle traffic to deal with—he might have said that who I will be is a question I should never stop asking. Or answering.

I think he might have reminded me that the world is big, and there are lands and people and stories beyond the horizon and as close as my new city.

Perhaps he would have promised that each time I dare to open my life to them, I will learn a little more of who I am.

—Margaret Wynn Chen
Seattle

AUTHOR'S NOTE

In researching my novel *Hitch,* I'd gone to the National Archives and Records Administration facility in Seattle to look at Civilian Conservation Corps material. Susan Karren, a NARA archivist generous and enthusiastic in her wish to convey the wealth of material there, introduced me to the Chinese immigration files. When she did, I knew I had my next book.

An author writes for many reasons, including the opportunity to explore other times and lives. Sometimes this means looking back to a slim slice of history, as I did in developing the story of Fai-yi Li. Sometimes what you find reminds you that the issues of today are not new ones. Certainly immigration isn't. What has varied over the centuries is who the immigrants are, why and how they have come here, what our laws say about their status, and how—or whether—they are welcomed.

A need for labor—particularly inexpensive labor—has fueled many immigration waves. It did in the nineteenth century, when muscle power was needed to dig mines and to lay the tracks of a fast-growing network of railroads. By the 1880s, however, the United States was struggling through an economic depression, and Chinese and American workers were in competition for jobs.

Violence erupted in places—a riot in Rock Springs, Wyoming, took twenty-eight Chinese lives; the Snake River Massacre in Hell's Canyon, Oregon, took another thirty-one. Up and down the West Coast, arguments raged between citizens who wanted to protect immigrants from what was called the Driving Out and those who wanted the immigrants, especially the Chinese immigrants, gone.

Meanwhile, shape was being given to laws that would collectively result in the years from 1882 to 1943 becoming known as the Exclusion Era.

The first of these laws, passed in 1882, suspended immigration of Chinese laborers for ten years and also established groups—teachers, students, merchants, and travelers—that would be exempt. The Geary Act in 1892 continued the suspension and also required Chinese to register and obtain certificates verifying their right to be in the United States. Other laws added more provisions, and court decisions modified interpretations. And then, in 1904, another act extended indefinitely all Chinese exclusion laws then in effect.

Chinese immigration did not completely stop during the four decades that followed. There were those who could immigrate because of exempt status. There were those who could come here because they had a parent or spouse who was a legal resident. And there were the paper sons.

The 1906 San Francisco earthquake and fire destroyed the Hall of Records there, with its documentation of births, marriages, and deaths. This opened the way for immigrants to claim they'd actually been born on United States soil, which would make them and their children citizens. And it fueled the growing practice by which a Chinese man who resided in the United States would claim to have living in China more children than he actually had and apply for permission to bring them here. He might then give away or sell the extra "slots," perhaps to relatives or friends, perhaps to strangers. On paper, he would be their father; a person taking such a slot would be a paper son. And the slots almost always did go to males rather than to females.

Immigration officials watched for these schemes, conducting detailed interrogations that were designed to expose someone who was falsely claiming to be from a particular place or family. Whether an immigrant was a paper son or a true one, his fear that he might be deported because he answered a question incorrectly was a valid one. Transcripts of interrogations that ask questions such as "How are the houses arranged in your village?" "How many in each row?" "Is there a wall?" are part of the archived files.

The Exclusion Era laws, which focused on Chinese immigration but also affected other groups of immigrants, including Japanese, Koreans, and Filipinos, were not lifted until 1943. Then, in the middle of World War II, with China being an ally, President Franklin D. Roosevelt signed the Act to Repeal the Chinese Exclusion Acts, to Establish Quotas, and for Other Purposes. It ended the Exclusion Era and set the stage for future legislation that would gradually ease remaining restrictions.

However, exploring and writing about other times and lives is not confined to looking into the past and examining the present in light of it. It's also about trying to capture a changing present in a way that invites speculation about tomorrow.

When I first went to work in a newsroom, I sat at a typewriter. Not long after, the Underwoods were gone, replaced by computers, but a reporter's work stayed the same: talk to people, dig through files, go out and see for oneself. Write up what was gleaned so that readers would have the information they needed to understand events and to make decisions. *The Missoulian,* with its big pages and fat sections, was delivered every morning and was the first, main source of news for most folks in western Montana.

Now the days of the *newspaper*—meaning only inked lines on paper—are gone, and the industry—print, broadcast, and even online—is struggling through a painful rebirth. The Internet offers reporters research possibilities unimaginable when I sat before that typewriter, but it also means that the business side of a news organization must find ways to compete in a marketplace where new forms of competition seem to appear overnight. I've tried, in writing Maggie's story, to capture a newsroom straddling the change from traditional to electronic format or some combination of the two.

And I've tried, also, to say that although—like Harrison—I hope newsprint will stream across press rollers for years to come, what's really important is that the news itself continues to be covered honestly and completely. As he tells Maggie, a democracy depends on a population that knows what's going on, and people depend on good, dedicated journalists to find out and pass it along.

—Jeanette Ingold, 2009

ACKNOWLEDGMENTS

Thank you, Mea Andrews, Kathi Appelt, Carol Brown, Tom C. Brown, Beverly Chin, Peggy Christian, Sneed B. Collard III, Rebecca Kai Dotlich, Jodee Fenton, Karen Grove, Elizabeth Harding, Kimberly Willis Holt, Kurt Ingold, Susan H. Karren, Wendy Norgaard, Dorothy Hinshaw Patent, Lola Schaefer, Lynn Schwanke, and Bruce Weide.

References and Suggestions for Learning More

BOOKS

Chang, Iris. *The Chinese in America: A Narrative History.* New York: Viking/Penguin Group, 2003.

Kung, S. W. *Chinese in American Life: Some Aspects of Their History, Status, Problems, and Contributions.* Seattle: University of Washington Press, 1962.

Ling, Huping. *Surviving on the Gold Mountain: A History of Chinese American Women and Their Lives.* Albany: State University of New York Press, 1998.

Sung, Betty Lee. *Mountain of Gold: The Story of the Chinese in America.* New York: The Macmillan Company, 1967.

Tung, William L. *The Chinese in America 1820–1973: A Chronology & Fact Book.* Dobbs Ferry, New York: Oceana Publications, 1974.

DOCUMENT

NATIONAL ARCHIVES AND RECORDS ADMINISTRATION
Reference Information Paper 99, compiled by Lowell, Waverly B. *Chinese Immigration and Chinese in the United States: Records in the Regional Archives of the National Archives and Records Administration,* 1996.

INTERNET SOURCES

Angel Island Association in cooperation with the California Department of Parks and Recreation homepage with link to Immigration Station material.
www.angelisland.org

Association for Education in Journalism and Mass Communication homepage.
aejmc.org

Associated Press homepage.
www.ap.org

Harvard University open collection of Exclusion Era–related material.
ocp.hul.harvard.edu/immigration/themes-exclusion.html

Library of Congress homepage.
www.loc.gov

National Archives and Records Administration homepage.
www.archives.gov

National Park Service Ellis Island homepage.
www.nps.gov/elis

Newseum homepage, with links to museum activities and teacher and student resources.
www.newseum.org

Newspaper Association of America homepage, with links to NAA Foundation programs including Newspapers in Education (NIE) and the Youth Editorial Alliance (YEA).
www.naa.org

NewspaperIndex.com homepage, with links to newspapers and front pages from around the world.
www.newspaperindex.com

Radio Television Digital News Association.
www.rtnda.org

University of California's Calsphere collection of primary sources homepage with link to Chinese Exclusion Act documents and photographs.
www.calisphere.universityofcalifornia.edu

University of Washington libraries digital collections homepage.
content.lib.washington.edu